T0095705

Garner's Resolve

Garner's Resolve

John Veary

authorHOUSE®

AuthorHouse™
1663 Liberty Drive
Bloomington, IN 47403
www.authorhouse.com
Phone: 1-800-839-8640

This is a work of fiction. All of the characters, names, incidents, organizations, and dialogue in this novel are either the products of the author's imagination or are used fictitiously.

Published by AuthorHouse   05/15/2013

ISBN: 978-1-4817-8676-8 (sc)
ISBN: 978-1-4817-8677-5 (e)

Contents

Acknowledgements

My thanks to a number of my family for their support and encouragement over the many months of me writing my book, and going on about being a "Famous Author".

Special thanks goes to my nephew Ben German for his interest and support in the early stages, offering constructive criticism and ideas.

Thanks to my wife Jean for her patience and assistance as my prime pre-publication reader.

Thanks to my children, Mark, Sean, and particularly Claire who also read my chapters as they were produced.

My grandsons Andrew and Christopher who both played their part in encouraging me, and special thanks to Christopher for the brilliant book cover design.

And I must not forget Harry Tinoco who perhaps was my first "publisher" (You know what I mean, Harry).

Finally, many many thanks go to my son-in-law, Bob Eady, for his help and his patience in getting my book out there.

This book is dedicated to my grandchildren, Emma, Andrew, Christopher and Stephen.

Prologue/Synopsis

Ron Garner, ex-Soldier and recent resident of HM Prisons, resolves to get his daughter to safety following a World Wide Pandemic that has thrown the UK into a state of uncontrolled terror.

Collecting two other vulnerable people on the way he encounters danger and mystery before reaching his destination, but even then with an old adversary appearing, his story does not end there.

Global Pandemic

Global "world-wide, all embracing"

Pandemic "(of disease) of world-wide distribution"

There had been fears of a Global Pandemic for many years, particularly the latter half of the twentieth century, when man began to monitor and study new forms of Influenza.

There was indeed a complacency within some major nations although the European countries and the American continent set up scientific groups dedicated to the study and foretelling (where at all possible) of any such threats.

Vaccines were even prepared and stock-piled for use against new and relatively unknown types of diseases, financed by concerned authorities who realized the real horror of a world-wide epidemic.

John Veary

But there was always those territories that, for whatever reason, did very little or nothing at all, and it was somewhere within those areas that the new strain was born and was soon to sweep the whole world.

The Epidemic

Nobody knew how or exactly where it started, but the virus killed millions throughout the Far East and Europe before it's terrible attack on the United Kingdom that Spring.

The speed in which the virus attacked and spread was terrifying and threw the populations of nations into full scale panic, making control difficult and law and order practically impossible.

At first the symptoms were like any other flu strain, with the patient experiencing severe headaches, high temperature, then fever.

This was followed by hard lumps appearing all over the body, that then weeped copiously with pus.

The patient then had trouble breathing and fluid built up in the lungs.

Usually at this stage the patient died, in terrible discomfort and agony.

In a few cases a patient would come through all of this, but would have their mind affected and become insane, and in some cases have unusual incredible strength.

The Insanity was of a peculiar type, for patients who had come this route would now interact with each other in a social group, but would attack and kill those who had for some reason not been affected by the virus.

There were some of the population that had for some strange reason not yet been affected in any way, and very few who had suffered the virus in a mild way, like Ron Garner, and had come through it with a now natural immunity to it.

Introduction to Terror

They watched as she timidly moved down the deserted High Street.

The girl, age about twenty, had an expression of fear as she continued to glance about, not really knowing what she should expect to see.

She only knew what she had heard.

Rumours. Talk of mad people. People made mad by the strange killer virus that had swept the country, decimating the population and leaving communities without any real law and order.

This was the first time that the girl had ventured out from the small terraced council house where she lived alone with her widowed mother.

They had been alone for years since her father had died suddenly from a heart attack.

Her mother depended on her and the girl had been forced to leave the house as they were running out of food.

She had heard neighbours talking of shortages many days ago, but since then all of their neighbours had disappeared.

So, nervously she had left her mother alone and was now heading for the supermarket that was at the end of the High Street.

The girl had not seen a soul, and was becoming more and more nervous.

The three men and one woman now hiding from the girl in a shop front across the street, looked at each other with leering expressions, their eyes bloodshot and with watery blood running from the lower eyelids.

Each of them drooled copious amounts of thick saliva, running down over their jaws and onto their chests.

Their hair was unkempt and their teeth stained with the blackness of old blood.

The four made their move.

Across the street the girl became aware of their presence and she turned to look at them, her heart beating wildly with fear.

With terror in her eyes at the sight of them the girl attempted to scream but nothing came out.

She could not even run.

Her legs had turned to jelly.

She froze, totally terror stricken.

Then they were upon her, pulling her in all directions, tearing her clothing from her until she lay wearing the remnants of her torn undergarments.

Then, as the biggest of the men knelt over her, the girl's heart, weak like her father's, mercifully gave out and she died before the man's inhuman strength began to tear her arms from her body.

Within minutes the girl's now naked body was mutilated beyond recognition, arms torn off, then the head which was thrown away, then each leg was torn from the torso as the foursome wrenched and pulled like mad dogs would a rabbit.

Only then did the group quieten down and they slunk off, back into the shop that they had sprung from, and they sat in their corners chewing on the fresh bloody fleshy limbs that they had just won.

Chapter 1

The prison walls stood tall and imposing.

Newly built, the light brown brickwork gave a false impression of friendliness, hiding the bleak conditions within.

At this point in time the walls stood towering over very quiet and unusual surroundings.

There was a slight breeze, blowing some litter and dust in swirls at the open gates.

The small office-come-reception just inside the gates was empty and, like the whole area, there was not a living soul in sight.

An open door creaked rhythmically as the breeze worked it's way into the empty building.

There was usually a very busy road outside the prison, a dual carriageway that linked Woolwich with Thamesmead, but for many days now no vehicles had passed by.

John Veary

A black cat, scrawny and with matted hair, crept from the shrubbery that grew beside the road and quickly ran into the prison yard, disappearing into the building via the creaking door.

Nobody challenged it.

The cat, it's nose twitching in it's hunt for food, made it's way up some stairs and began to walk casually along a corridor.

Still no-one appeared, or made a sound to deter the cat's progress.

The cat stopped and peered around the open door to an empty room.

It raised it's head and sniffed, but nothing tempted it to move further into the room.

It padded further along the corridor then paused as it became aware of some evidence of man emitting from a room some yards ahead.

The animal snarled and the hair on it's arched back rose as it heard a voice, then smelt the sweat of humans.

The cat turned and ran swiftly back along the corridor, down the stairs and out of the building.

He heard a voice, saying his name. It seemed distant, and with an urgent request.

Through his dull and foggy mind came the sound of a tired and despairing voice, "Garner . . . c'mon man . . . wake up".

Ron Garner roused himself from the slumber of exhaustion that had followed the deep bout of intense fever.

"What? What's up?" his parched mouth and throat restricting his question to a coarse rasping.

He tried to lick his lips but his mouth allowed him no saliva.

"C'mon man, try to sit up. Here . . . I'll help you". The desperation in the weak voice came again and through blurred eyes Garner made out the pock marked ravaged features of Mr. Macey, the senior 'screw' on Garner's block.

As the burly figure attempted to lift him upwards, Garner gradually had memories of his situation.

He was serving time for his part in a robbery that went very wrong.

For the moment Garner could not remember how long he had been here.

He did remember the sudden bout of flu.

Or was it?

There had been the terrible weakness, the pain and the skin eruptions, then the fever.

They had moved him from his cell to the small prison hospital, but that seemed ages ago.

He had no idea how long.

A cool glass was pressed against his dry lips.

Then, beautiful sweet water was running down his chin as Mr. Macey attempted to help him take some of the delicious fluid between his lips.

Garner swallowed.

It tasted like nectar from heaven.

Reminded him of a time in the middle East when, after days of hiding from an enemy, he had been given such deliciously cool and sweet water.

Garner forced his eyes, heavy and still aching from days of enforced sleep, to open wider and he saw more clearly the dishevelled haggard face, as the older man hunched over him.

Mr. Macey looked terrible. His face was red and blotchy. He had the beginnings of dark swellings on his neck.

Usually the smartest of prison officers, Ted Macey, a ranking man of twenty years prison experience, had no tie on and his usually pristine white shirt, now creased and soiled, was agape at the throat revealing his upper chest that also now displayed the dark swellings.

His florid features were bathed in a sheen of feverish perspiration and he lowered his head to rest his face on the bed at Garner's side.

Garner tried to sit up but was suddenly too weak.

He fell back and fell into a deep slumber again.

Ted Macey, his fifty year old heart weakened by his recent exertions and anxieties, gasped and choked before he felt the terrific pain that pounded his chest, and he fell forward, dying there as he hunched across the still form of one of his recent charges.

Chapter 2

The day was now sunny bright, after a dark cloudy start and a heavy downpour.

Birds were singing and chattering in the trees as Sister Juliet drove into the long curving driveway that led up to the small convent.

Nothing else stirred in this quiet leafy suburban avenue close to Blackheath Village.

Laying back from the roadway, hidden behind tall lime trees, was the old converted Victorian vicarage, now the convent called St.Jude's.

Sister Juliet, a twenty year old novice sister drew the ten year old Ford to a stop and emerged from the car, an exhausted expression on her pretty face.

Sister Juliet had been to another small convent in South London to seek assistance for her and the one other remaining colleague, seventy-three year old sister Martha.

For some weeks now the sisters, under the guidance of the frail Sister Frances, the most senior Nun, had been attempting to nurse patients suffering from the terrible sickness that had spread throughout the world.

But she had found that the source of her hope was deserted and had turned back with a heavy heart.

Standing beside the car Sister Juliet listened to the peaceful sounds of the birds and she smiled blissfully.

Oh, if only God could make it so beautiful again, she thought.

She realised how humid it had become and her long garments felt heavy about her body.

A sheen of perspiration was on her forehead and her top lip.

She wearily made her way up to the front entrance and let herself in.

Upon entering the cool dark hallway sister Juliet was met by the sister Martha who was very disappointed to hear that no help was at hand.

"How are our patients?" Sister Juliet asked the old lady.

Martha's head dropped and she crossed herself before answering, "We have lost another two, and the poor things in the ward have become strangely quiet since the introduction of that strange foreigner yesterday."

They had, just days before, been trying to save two sick people upstairs in a special hospital room in the attic, but the two sick patients had died while Juliet was away that morning.

Sister Juliet smiled, "That's not a bad thing, is it?" she said, referring of course to the quietness among the small group of post-sickness patients who had survived the fever only to become strange inhuman beings with a madness and a terrible strength, needing a regular sedative to calm them, given to them in the water that they continually thirsted for.

And now they were contained downstairs in the vast cellar area, and behind large wooden doors.

Sister Martha looked puzzled, then said, "Oh, I don't know. They are quite strange, come and see"

The two black clad women walked side by side down to the cellar area of the small building to where Sister Frances, since deceased, had organised a secure room for the poor demented beings that had succumbed to the strange extremes after their attempts at healing them had failed.

"Poor Sister Frances meant well of these poor souls, and she prayed for them before she died" Sister Martha said.

Sister Frances had passed away in her sleep.

Natural causes at least, both surviving women agreed.

As the nuns approached the room, the strange hubbub that usually rumbled from within ceased and the sisters stopped at the large solid doors.

Both women cocked their heads to listen as a disconcerting quietness prevailed from within.

The Sisters looked at each other, puzzled expressions on their faces.

Sister Juliet slid a viewing panel sideways and peered into the dim expanse of the ward.

"They are strangely quiet" she agreed.

Ten adults, five women and five men, of all ages, stood together facing the door with quizzical looks on their scarred and abscess ridden faces, but all were standing quietly as a woman who had her back to the door faced them.

Sister Juliet recognised the woman as the patient who had arrived a week ago pleading for help in a strangely accented voice.

As with all of their patients they had attempted to help, the woman got over the fierce fever that beset people during the initial stages of the sickness.

But, once again, the evil virus won and one of the last decisions of Sister Frances was to have this poor woman sedated and moved into the cellar ward with the others.

There was always the faint hope that rescue would come and with it some form of cure for the sufferers.

The woman's blonde hair was matted and she seemed to be controlling the others with soft words and whispering and the movement of her head.

Sister Martha placed her head close to Juliet's and saw the same scene.

"See. She seems to have some influence with them. Has God sent her here to help us?" and she crossed herself again.

Sister Juliet frowned as she continued to watch the woman's odd control.

Then the woman turned quickly to face the door and Sister Juliet cried out with fear as she now saw the ravaged hideous features that glared at her.

The terrible sickness had now begun to eat the woman's face away.

A skeletal face that was now covered with gaping sores and abscess, that pus dribbled from slowly.

The foreign woman screeched and rushed at the door and sister Juliet stepped quickly away and closed the viewing panel, a cold sensation rushing through her slim body.

Sister Juliet shivered, fearing that the Devil had arrived and would spring free of his imprisonment.

She too made the cross of her faith and both nuns knelt and began to pray loudly.

There was a crescendo of noise from within the ward and the door shook as the occupants began to batter it with heavy pieces of furniture.

Heavy wooden pews, handled with inhuman strength, were used as battering rams and the kneeling sisters watch with awe as the door shook in it's frame, and then began to splinter at the panels.

Sister Juliet helped old Martha to her feet and as the couple began to retreat back along the passage towards the stairs, the door suddenly split and was then torn from it's hinges.

Both sisters stopped in their tracks and turned to face the madness that rushed from the ward towards them.

"God have mercy!" Sister Juliet cried loudly as Sister Martha was beaten to her knees first by three women wielding heavy pieces of broken furniture.

And then Sister Juliet was dragged to the ground by four of the men.

Screaming for mercy and praying out loud Martha was beaten to death, her head broken and bloodied.

Juliet survived another two minutes as her clothing was torn from her and then her white form was clawed at and bitten before huge chunks of her flesh was torn from her slim body.

Her pitiful cries to God ceased as she had her jugular bitten through by the blonde foreigner, and sister Juliet died.

Chapter 3

Nurse Elizabeth Ritchie, thirty-four years of age, but feeling more like sixty-four at this moment, woke from the nap that she was having in the small office along from the prison ward, and stretching her arms above her head she stood up.

She looked over at the clock on the wall.

God! She had overslept.

She had better relieve old Ted and see how their one remaining patient was.

An attractive Irish lass, Elizabeth, or Lizzie to her friends, had been seconded to the prison from the local hospital when the virus had caused such concern, and the prison inmates began to drop like flies from it's terrible onslaught.

Gradually even the staff became ill and disappeared, and eventually only she and Ted Macey were left at the prison.

Feeling isolated and very scared Lizzie continued with her job, even though she or her companion had no contact with the outside world, and there had been no sign of any relief.

She had depended on Ted Macey, and she knew that he was becoming ill too, but he insisted that help would come and Lizzie had gone along with that.

All of the patients had died except for one.

She had helped Ted to move the corpses to another room, and had concentrated on trying to keep this last patient alive.

Automatically Lizzie straightened her small head covering, and checked herself in the small wall mirror.

The face she saw was pale, framed by thick auburn hair that fell to her shoulders, and there were the small rings of tiredness under her eyes.

Going over to the small hand basin she splashed a little water over her face and dried herself on the tissue towelling.

Feeling a little better now she left the room and made her way along to the isolation ward.

As she entered the room her first sight was of Ted hunched over the bed.

The man had collapsed on to a chair beside the bed and appeared to have fallen asleep.

Glancing at the patient who was apparently in a deep sleep, snoring gently, Lizzie walked over and tapped Ted on the shoulder.

"Ted. Sorry I'm late . . . . I overslept".

"Ted?" Lizzie now became worried as there was no response at all.

Lizzie leaned closer and looked at his face.

The way it was contorted and the fact that his eyes were open suggested the worst.

"Oh no . . . . no". She cried and putting her fingers to his throat she felt for a pulse.

None.

Ted Macey was quite dead.

The patient groaned and Lizzie moved over between the dead man and the almost living.

"Ron? Mr. Garner?" she said quietly, leaning close to his ear.

Garner stirred and his eyes opened slightly.

He licked his lips.

"Water, please", he managed to say.

Lizzie could see the water stains on the front of his pyjamas and on the bed covers, and the plastic cup still clutched in Ted's hand.

She went over to a water dispenser and filled another cup with the cool fluid, then she returned to the patient.

She helped him to sip the water.

"He's dead, is'nt he?" Garner said, looking down at the still figure beside them.

"Yes" Lizzie replied, tears in her green eyes, "Poor man. He must have been quite ill. It was his heart, I think".

"Where are the others?" he then asked as he glanced around the small ward.

This was a good sign.

Lizzie felt that at least this one, her last patient, had made it through the terrible unknown fever caused by the virulent virus.

So far, anyway.

He certainly appeared to be more with it than any other one that she had nursed during the recent weeks.

"Well . . . ." Lizzie seemed unsure of her next words, ". . . . I'm sure help will arrive here soon. So relax. Try to get more rest, and I'll move Mr. Macey".

But Garner had seen the tears starting in her green eyes.

Feeling helpless he watched as the young woman left the room, returning in minutes with a wheelchair.

Silently she struggled to get the heavy corpse from the bedside and onto the wheelchair, but she did it, probably due to the training that she had as a student nurse some years ago.

Garner, laying back, but with slitted eyes watching, followed the nurse's every move, and feeling quite helpless and frustrated.

Lizzie wheeled the dead man from the room and Garner heard her as she walked down the corridor.

He heard a door shut and then the sounds of footsteps as she approached his room again.

Pulling up a chair Lizzie sat beside the bed and assisted him in taking in more water.

She checked his pulse and found it to be normal.

His fever had disappeared and apart from looking flushed he looked a hundred per cent better.

She sat with him during the next two hours, during which he fell asleep once again.

All was deadly quiet.

No sounds, except for the distant creaking of a door blowing in the breeze and her patients soft snoring.

Lizzie lowered her head to the bed.

Still holding Garner's wrist with her hand she began to weep softly.

What was going to happen to them?

Would help come?

She felt so alone, and so very desperate.

In his dreams, and just as in every dream before, Garner searched anxiously for his little girl, his Sammy.

Tossing and grunting quietly he saw the slim fair haired youngster flitting from one scene to another.

He chased after her, mutely calling her name and every time she faded from his view and his heart grew heavy and he wept.

Chapter 4

It was a quiet road with well maintained 1930's style semi-detached houses on either side.

On this particular evening an open topped sports car had quietly run up the empty driveway of one of these houses and the occupant, a tall athletic dark haired man, had swiftly forced his way into the house.

Searching the house he found that it was empty, as so many others were since the outbreak of the strange and lethal epidemic.

With little respect for the owner's personal items, that was if the owners were still alive, the man rummaged through the drawers in all of the rooms, slipping a few valuable items into his pockets.

Finding a photograph album the man thumbed through the pages leering at the pictures of a well formed woman posing on holiday in a bikini.

Tearing one of these out he slipped that into the inside pocket of his bomber jacket.

He then poured himself a glass of single malt that he found in the corner cupboard of the large front lounge, and spread himself out on the leather settee, sipping the rich malty scotch and his eyes darting about the room in the hunt for anything else that he could help himself to.

Then, still sipping the scotch, he rose and stood silently in the bay window and his black piercing eyes searched the houses opposite, one in particular.

It was becoming dark now and after another glass of the golden nectar his slipped out of the house and ran quickly across the road and up to the bay windows of the house that interested him.

He knew this house well.

Many the time some years previous he had occasion to visit the occupants.

The whole neighbourhood was deathly quiet as the man expertly forced one of the windows before climbing into the front lounge.

Silently the man went from room to room, turning out cupboards and drawers, obviously searching for a particular thing.

Finally, and with a string of expletives, he stood in the lounge and lit a strong smelling cheroot.

He noticed a framed photograph of a man and woman together with a small girl, and with a look of hatred on his handsome face he dropped the frame onto the carpet and ground it to fragments under his heavy boots.

Then muttering hatefully, "I'll find it, and I'll find you, you bastard". The man left the house by the front door, slamming it shut as he went.

Chapter 5

It was evening when he woke again.

He did not know until Lizzie told him, but he had slept for a further twenty-four hours.

Lizzie bustled around him and she disappeared down the hall to her small office where she set about preparing him some food.

She was unable to heat anything as there was no electricity and had not been for some days now, so she opened a can of vegetable soup and poured it cold into a small pan.

Lizzie had a small portable gas ring, attached via a rubber pipe to a gas tap that sat in a corner of the worktop and was partly hidden by various other kitchen utensils.

She turned the gas tap and was surprised to hear the hiss of gas, so lighting it quickly with some matches found nearby, she proceeded to heat the soup.

Garner was actually feeling famished and when he began to smell the aroma of hot food his saliva glands ran freely.

He felt stronger and he managed to sit up higher in the bed, making himself comfortable and ready for whatever it was the nurse was preparing.

He listened and looked around.

It was so strange.

There were none of the familiar sounds that he had become accustomed to in the time that he had spent here, in prison.

And also very strange was the absence of the 'screws' and it worried him now that he remembered recent events, and seeing the nurse wheel away Mr. Macey, who was obviously very dead.

Lizzie returned with some hot vegetable soup, and tinned salmon sandwiches.

The bread was days old but that did not matter to Garner at this time.

She had made enough for two and she sat beside the bed, and they both ate heartily.

Garner did not realise just how hungry he was and he excused himself to Lizzie for bolting the food quickly.

He belched, closing his eyes with the pleasure of having a full belly.

Or that was how he felt now.

"What's your name?" he asked her.

She introduced herself then answered a multitude of questions that he threw at her.

It had been over two weeks since he gone down with the virus, and now Lizzie brought him up to date, her face becoming strained and serious as she related the state of the country, and as far as she knew, the whole world.

Apparently it was rare for anyone to pull through the illness as he seemed to have, but there had been rumours of many ways the virus had affected the population.

Garner looked at her with a serious expression on his face.

"Thanks" he said.

Lizzie lifted her face to meet his gaze.

"Thank you for your time spent trying to help me" Garner said sincerely to her.

"It's my job . . . profession" Lizzie replied, a red blush momentarily spreading over her freckled cheeks.

"Is there anyone left here at all?" he continued.

Lizzie shook he head, "No. Just us now . . . I . . . I . . . don't know if . . . when help might come".

She wept, then excused herself, straightening her back and wiping her eyes.

Garner remained silent for a while and then he spoke, and with a quiet authority, prompting Lizzie to believe that he had been sometime in his past, a man of some strength and action.

Over the following days and weeks she was to find out just how strong and intelligent he could be.

He told her that they would remain in the prison this one last night, and that she must rest and try to sleep, 'recharging their batteries' he said, then tomorrow he would find appropriate clothing and they would leave the prison and attempt to seek out some help.

At least try to find others, who like them were survivors.

But most of all she found that Garner was resolved to finding his young daughter, whatever her situation.

Lizzie felt somewhat safer and more comfortable with this man who for whatever reason had done something illegal and had earned time as a resident in Her Majesty's prison.

She went to her small room and, pulling a blanket over herself, she fell asleep on the single bunk.

Chapter 6

The young girl's eyes searched the road outside as she stood beside the bay window.

Her mother had been gone for four days now and the girl was naturally worried sick.

She had done what her mother had ordered and had kept herself out of sight in the secret room, but after seven days the youngster had ventured out to look for any sign of her mother's return.

The girl was quite slim and tall for her age and she had tried to keep herself tidy by regularly washing and changing her clothing, but the dark rings around her eyes and the tear run cheeks showed how worried she had become.

It had been during last night that she had thought that her mother had returned.

Woken from a fitful sleep by a noise in the house the girl had crept to the secret doorand had listened first before opening the door, as advised by her mother.

She had cringed, her heart beating wildly, when she heard the rasping cough of a stranger.

Then, due to an acute sense of smell, the youngster detected the acrid smell of tobacco, and strong cigarettes.

She had quietly closed the door and had crept back to the secret room.

The girl returned to her bunk and snuggled up under a thick blanket, fearing that the stranger might discover her.

Her mouth became dry and she trembled in fear, tears running once again from her blue eyes.

Then, it became quiet and she prayed that the person had left the house, and she dozed on and off until dawn.

She rose and relieved herself in the special toilet that was part of her secret place, then she ventured once again to the door of her hiding place.

There was no sound.

The youngster stood by the door, listening hard before gradually edging the door open.

The front room of the house was empty although the girl could still smell the cigarette smoke.

Believing that the stranger had gone the girl had crept over to the bay window and she had cried as she looked down the road to the junction.

If, and when her mother returned it would be from that direction.

Her mother had gone to find others that might be of help and advice, and she had obviously become delayed, or worse.

And so the youngster wept, and after minutes agonising at the window she returned to the secret room.

Chapter 7

It was dawn when Garner, now dressed in a set of navy overalls and a thick roll-neck sweater, woke Lizzie.

He allowed her time for her ablutions then told her of his plan to make for his old home where he hoped to find his estranged wife, and more importantly, his young daughter.

They left the stark prison walls behind them and made their way along desolate streets passing abandoned vehicles and goods, and even a few burnt out buildings.

They passed a group of five bloated bodies covered in flies that seem to rise and attack them as they hurried past.

There had been, not far from the prison, a major bus terminal, and as they approached it Garner and Lizzie became aware of the strong acrid smell of burnt rubber and metal.

The bus station and the buses were totally burnt out.

"That happened last week" offered Lizzie, "There weren't any fire services around to see to it".

He managed a smile, "I wasn't planning on getting a bus home, anyway" he grunted.

Lizzie, not yet used to his humour, looked at him with a strange expression of disbelief.

He saw the strange look and said, "Only joking. C'mon, let's keep going". And he led her away and up a hill in the direction he had originally planned.

There were a few cars left at the roadside but each one was locked, so he decided to be patient and hope to find the right vehicle soon, and the method to start it.

The weather was now sunny but quite fresh with a chilly breeze, but their exertions kept them warm.

Garner knew where he was making for and walked with a sense of purpose, his muscles now aching considerably since his recent enforced time spent in bed.

They were crossing an area of common land when a voice shouted from behind them.

"Hey. Hold on". It was a man's voice.

The stranger, dressed in jogging pants and sports top, sprinted up to them, a smile on his thin face.

Aged about thirty he appeared to be fit and healthy although he had dark rings under his eyes and a few scabs on his face and hands.

"Ai'nt I glad to see you" he grinned broadly as he walked along with them, "I'm Roger. Been on me own for days now. Was ill, but feel OK now".

Roger plodded along beside them, his thin reedy voice continually ranting on about how he was fending for himself, and bragging about how he had fought with three 'mad' characters and had defeated them, and he brandished a wicked looking sheath knife.

"Cut 'em up good", and he laughed.

Garner grunted, looking at the man with a disdained expression, not really believing him.

Roger seemed to sulk at this reaction and became quiet.

After a while, walking in silence, Lizzie noticed how Roger kept looking at her.

Garner had forged ahead a little, leaving Lizzie closer to the strange man.

She felt uncomfortable and moved to walk with Garner in between herself and this stranger.

Each time she caught Roger looking at her he was licking his lips and had a strange look on his face.

They had reached the edge of the common when it happened.

Suddenly Roger brought his knife into view and slashed out at Garner.

Garner was faintly aware of the sudden movement and he automatically flinched but also moved his body to one side.

Unprepared, and out of practice, he swung backwards to ward off the flailing weapon, and stumbled on the edge of a kerbside, and fell heavily in the road.

Roger lashed out with his foot and hit Garner in the stomach, winding him and causing him to double up.

Roger, a terrible insane look on his face, now turned to the petrified nurse and she tried to run from him but was caught by his flailing arm and a tremendous pained screamed through her body as the knife sliced easily through her jacket and penetrated her back, just below the right shoulder.

She fell to the road and the mad man threw himself on her, sitting on her bleeding back.

Laying there with her face pressed to the tarmac, Lizzie passed out with the pain and the terror that had suddenly engulfed her.

Grinning insanely Roger lifted Lizzie's head by dragging her long hair upwards in his free hand, ready to slice her throat with the knife, when Garner dived on to him and wrestled him away from the prone woman.

Garner's training now came into use and in seconds he had gripped the mad man by the head and had twisted it expertly, hearing the spine crack as the neck was broken.

He threw the limp body to one side and scrambled over to Lizzie.

Fearing the worst he stared in disbelief at the copious amount of her blood spreading beneath her inert body.

Looking around he saw that there was nobody around who might help him, so he clawed at her jacket, lifting it to reveal the bloody mess at the top of uniform.

With strength gained out of desperation he ripped her clothing open to discover the ugly and apparently deep knife wound with her blood seeping easily from it.

Standing up, Garner looked about, searching for something to use in an attempt to stem the flow of blood.

He used the knife and cut the sports top from the mad man and he tore it into strips and padding.

He next half an hour Garner spent applying the cloths and finally felt happy that the bleeding had slowed.

Lizzie had regained consciousness now and she moaned softly, a throbbing pain causing tears to run from her tired eyes.

Garner found himself comforting her.

He knelt down beside her, cradling her in his arms.

"Don't worry, love" He told her, "I'll sort something". And he lifted her closer to a wall that ran along the front of a fine looking Georgian house.

"Won't be a minute" he said and he slipped through a side gate and found his way to the back of the building.

Garner thought that he ought to knock before breaking in the back door.

There was no response so he forced the door with a spade that stood conveniently beside a shed.

He entered the house, passing through a large kitchen and searching the rooms.

As he entered the front parlour a familiar sickening odour beset his senses, and he knew before he saw it that there was a rotting body in the room.

Ignoring the sight of the unfortunate person, an aging woman laying on the floor, Garner noticed the wheelchair and quickly wheeled it from the room.

He sped out to the front of the house, unbolting and going out the front door, and found that Lizzie had passed out again.

Looking around Garner was still amazed at the quietness and the absence of people.

Raising Lizzie as gently as he could he put her in the wheelchair and returned to the house where he lay her on the settee in a cosy back room.

Then he went up to the bedrooms and returned with some pillows and blankets.

He made Lizzie as comfortable as possible.

Strange, he thought, the tables were now turned and it was his turn to nurse his nurse.

There were some tinned foods in the kitchen cupboards.

He turned the gas tap on the hob.

A little gas escaped, then . . . . nothing.

Looking around he spied the microwave oven buried by a heap of clothing.

Trying this he discovered that the electrical supply was not functioning.

Garner stood thinking for a moment then he searched the house, finally going down into a deep cellar where luckily he found some old camping equipment, including of all things a portable gas ring and a can of liquid gas.

He shook the can and was glad to find that it still held some fuel.

So returning to the kitchen he used the gas ring to warm up some soup and baked beans.

He ate hungrily, realising that his body was in need of plenty of sustenance to regain his lost strength.

There was bottled beer in the fridge, which also was not functioning, but he helped himself to it anyway, luxuriating in the sharp delicious taste of the amber nectar.

Lizzie groaned and he went to her.

It was now early afternoon and Garner was keen to get to his planned destination before dusk.

He searched the garage and found nothing.

The neighbouring garage was locked.

But using an iron bar that he had found alongside the garage, Garner broke in and discovered a gleaming new Volvo.

The keys were on display on a hook on the wall and he had no problem starting the vehicle and driving it out and into the road outside the house in which Lizzie lay.

Wrapped in the blanket, and with a pillow under her head, Lizzie was made as comfortable as he could make her, in the back of the car, then he started up and drove away.

Avoiding vehicles left in and across roads and junctions, he drove towards his home, and it took nearly an hour before he turned into the familiar road that led to his house.

He had not seen or heard any other human being on his journey and was now realising the enormity of his situation.

He pulled up in the drive of his house and sat in the car for a while, taking in his surroundings.

The house was a typical semi found in the city suburbs, and showed no sign of damage as indeed many others had on his way in.

Locking Lizzie in the car he approached the front door.

It was locked.

He knocked.

He rang the bell.

Nothing.

He never noticed that one of the bay windows had been forced.

Garner went down the side of the house and climbed over the side gate.

The back door, leading to the kitchen was also locked.

Smiling, Garner went down the long garden to the shed and found that the door was broken and open.

He entered the musty old shed, once his pride and joy.

His workshop.

Yes, it was there.

From a shelf above the shed door he took an old tobacco tin and found the spare keys he had left there months ago.

He hurried back to the side gate and unlocked it, then unlocked the kitchen door.

Within minutes he had Lizzie in the house and sleeping soundly in a bed upstairs.

There was no sign of his wife Freda, or Sammy.

But he did notice how the usually tidy rooms were now in some disarray.

Garner searched for some clue to his wife's, or his daughter's, whereabouts before sitting in an armchair and closing his eyes.

Then it came to him.

He knew where they could be.

Going over to the cupboard that was built under the stairs he opened the door and went inside.

Yes. The shelving at the back had been removed.

The tongue and grooved panelling appeared plain and uninteresting.

Garner put out a hand to touch it.

But suddenly the whole back panel was pulled back into a black void and his eyes blurred with tears as a slim scruffy fair haired teenage girl rushed out into his arms.

"Sammy . . . Sammy . . . . my baby . . . . my baby . . . ." he cried and held his daughter in a tight embrace.

Chapter 8

Ron Garner, now well into his forties, had always been a soldier.

He had joined the army as a teenager deciding to make the service his career.

Hi did well, attaining the heady rank of sergeant, and had spent the final four years of service as a member of the elite SAS group.

He had loved the army and only when he had been married for some years and the need arose for a financial situation allowing him to settle with his wife and their young child did he leave, and he took his pension.

Garner had met Freda in Hamburg during a spell of duty in Germany.

Freda was a qualified mid-wife and worked in the outskirts of Hamburg.

She had fallen for the well built young soldier who's thinning hairline was shaven giving him a rather fierce and intimidating look.

The lively blonde had captured his heart and they had married within two months of their meeting.

It was not all plain sailing.

Freda still hankered for the good life and quickly became bored with her soldier husband's routine life.

She was never aware of his service away when he was embroiled in secret SAS activities, usually in the Middle East.

They had a daughter, Samantha Jane, who they both doted on, but after a few years Freda began to stray, eventually leaving Garner for six months to live with her lover, one of Garner's colleagues, Corporal Harvey Rollison.

Rollison was an arrogant conceited man who Garner had never fully trusted, but he had been an integral part of the SAS unit, under Garner's command.

Freda had soon discovered her mistake and had come home to Garner and Sammy pleading for forgiveness.

He took her back for two reasons.

One. Sammy needed her mother.

Two. Garner still had feelings for her.

Not the same, but he felt that he could not totally let go.

So to satisfy her lust for an easy life he had agreed to leave the forces and take an early pension.

This worked for a while.

They had purchased the house through a mortgage and Sammy settled happily with her seemingly happy parents.

Garner got a job as a chauffeur and minder for a city gent, and things began to settle down.

Until.

Freda again became unsettled and unhappy with her lot.

Being a housewife and mother, doing shopping, housework, and the usual boring trek to and from Sammy's school was to her very boring, and she felt that she did not fit in with the other young mothers.

She started to spend.

Freda began to stay out late, with new friends that Garner was not too sure of.

He realised that their finances were beginning to dwindle and they were soon in debt.

Then there was the heart rending blow when Sammy had an accident when on her way home, alone, from school.

The youngster suffered severe head injuries, and she became partly mute.

Sammy had been nine years of age then.

It was then that Harvey Rollison had appeared once again in their lives.

He had rung Garner one evening and had proposed that they meet.

Curious but interested in the remark that Rollison had made about a financial advantage Garner had agreed and had met his old adversary in a nearby pub.

Rollison, and the two shady cronies he had with him, had put a proposition to Garner that at first he was dead against.

They suggested that he join them as a driver in a planned robbery.

At first he was totally furious and began to rise from the table that the four of them sat around, when Rolly (Rollison) suggested that his cut of the proceeds would amount to an unbelievable figure Garner had stayed and heard them out.

Grudgingly and meaning to participate only the once in such a daring and illegal task, he had agreed.

The upshot of it was that although the robbery went well as they cleverly took thousands of pounds worth of watches and jewellery from a well known West End store, during the getaway the two cronies were caught instantly by the police, and Garner, who had managed to escape and make it home with part of the proceeds, was eventually arrested at home.

Only the crafty Rollison got away.

During the brief time that he was at his house, before the police arrived, Garner handed a small blue velvet bag to Freda.

He impressed on her that she must hide the bag until he was free and able to use the contents, but after the trial and his imprisonment he heard no more of it.

Even now, sitting at home with Sammy cuddled up on his lap he did not think about the ill gotten treasure.

He was just so glad that he had found the youngster apparently safe and well.

The whole immediate district was so quiet.

There were no signs of any other humans, or animals.

Even cats and dogs were conspicuous by their absence.

And Garner was happy that his daughter knew little of the epidemic and it's effect on the population, and she appeared untouched in her own health.

Sammy was able to write and so he managed to get some information from her, how she had survived after Freda had

John Veary

gone out alone to try and find other people who, like her and Sammy, were isolated and apparently well.

Sammy had remained at home, waiting sometimes at the window and praying that her mother would return, but so far there had been no sign of her.

The youngster had survived on tinned food from the kitchen larder, and then had taken to sleeping and eating in the strange underground room that lay beneath their back garden, just as her mother had instructed.

Garner had discovered this room years ago when he was clearing out the area under the stairs before building additional shelving for storage.

The door, concealed behind a camouflaged facing of tongue and grooved timber, led down and into a narrow corridor that ran under the back kitchen area and under the lawned garden.

This corridor led to an iron door.

Garner found in time that a clever lighting system, driven by a small oil generator and with ventilation, lit the narrow pit and tunnel, and the lighting above the iron door.

He further discovered a dust envelope tucked behind a pipe that ran from the house and along the tunnel.

Inside this envelope was an eight figured number that turned out to be the combination required to open the iron door.

When he and Freda had purchased the house they had been told that the previous owner had been a well respected but quite eccentric scientist, a Professor George Smallwood, who had died at the house leaving it to a distant relative to dispose of.

So Garner imagined how the old man must have been so incensed by the ways of the modern world, and the way that the powerful nations were heading, that he had secretly had this underground shelter built.

Neighbours must have been intrigued and puzzled, annoyed as well during the period that the high panelling and temporary plastic roofing had hidden the construction.

From old invoices he found in the secret room Garner read that it had been built by a firm generally associated with government contacts in 1953.

This had occurred in the summer of that year and afterwards, after the garden had been re-landscaped, nobody would have guessed what lay beneath.

Prof. Smallwood had built in a clever system of ventilation that could be closed in the event of a nuclear attack.

He had also built in a large water tank for drinking water and hygiene, and also a supply of tinned foods.

There were some tools and torches, although batteries would be needed, and many other items that could be used in the possible event of isolation.

There was one comfortable bunk bed and two sleeping bags, blankets and pillows.

It was obvious that no one, even the estate agent who sold the house to Garner, were aware of this underground structure, and it's cleverly concealed entrance.

So now, while he relaxed a bit with Sammy, Garner was already planning to live in the secret chamber, moving the injured Lizzie down there as well, where both and his daughter could nurse her until she was well enough to be moved over a greater distance when he decided it was time to leave and search for some form of controlling authority and safety for him, Sammy, and now his new charge, Lizzie.

He was pleasantly surprised to find that Sammy was keen to help nurse Lizzie and he allowed her to spend time with the patient.

They stayed in the house, and in the underground chamber, for two weeks before he considered Lizzie was well enough to travel.

During this time the nurse's health improved although the wound in her back was slow to heal.

And during this period Garner had frequently watched from the bay window, hoping that Freda might suddenly appear and return to them.

He was really concerned for.

And it troubled him.

Lizzie had allowed him and Sammy to inspect the wound and, following his description of it, she had suggested that perhaps it should be stitched.

So under instruction from Lizzie, and using a simple needle and some black thread that Sammy gave him from her needlework box, Garner managed a crude stitching job, bringing the edges of the gaping, but clean, wound together.

Later he found that she was still somewhat weak, but her general demeanour was encouraging.

She and young Sammy had become friends and Garner smiled on noticing this, feeling content now that his daughter was relaxed and happy.

He had time to reflect on his life so far and he remembered his many satisfying years in the army.

Garner was a soldier.

Had always been, and a good one at that.

He remembered having the rare opportunity to fly a helicopter in the service.

He and Paul Graveney, a pilot on the base in Germany, became friends, and Paul would show Garner the planes controls and explain how they were used.

Paul knew that the soldier was champing at the bit to have a go but he stuck to the rules and only talked him through the flight procedures.

Then during one of their SAS sorties in a Middle East country the opportunity arose for Garner.

They had been surprised by an ambushing enemy and the helicopter was called in to evacuate the survivors.

As the aircraft landed the crew were all hit and badly wounded.

Sergeant Garner assumed command and had, with the guidance of his friend, the now seriously wounded pilot, been able to fly the helicopter off and back to base where he managed to land it safely.

For this he gained a commendation, and the heartfelt thanks of all of his comrades.

Following this, and when Paul Graveney returned to his duties, Garner was given a few unofficial flying lessons, until it became more difficult and the lessons ceased.

Paul was then posted back to the UK.

It was soon after this that Garner applied to leave the army and his contact with Paul and his chances to fly again stopped.

Now one of Garner's current ideas was to be able to get to a helicopter, and he considered making for the nearest airfield when they finally left the house.

In the time that they had remained in the secret chamber he had thought a lot about what he should do.

His priority was to get his daughter, and now Lizzie, to safety.

But it took him some days before he considered it sensible to aim for a secret military complex that he had become aware of during his SAS days.

It was possible that an authority and a control would be functioning there during these desperate days.

So having made his mind up he planned to move South Westwards as soon as Lizzie was fir enough to travel.

Whatever was to happen he resolved to get his daughter and Lizzie to a safe secure place as soon as possible.

By travelling over the route he had chosen after studying road maps of Southern England, he would pass a couple of airfields and maybe find the helicopter he dreamed of using.

But events were to force him to change his plan.

He began to leave the house at night and he built up a stock of petrol, in cans, by siphoning from newer type abandoned cars in his immediate area.

Garner planned to use the new Volvo that he had brought to the house, refilling it with petrol as they made their way towards his goal.

In a house immediately across the road from where Garner and the girl's were, a tall sinister figure watched, waiting for the right moment, chain smoking thin dark cheroots, and taking the odd short rest, sleeping in an armchair in the bay area where the windows faced Garner's house.

It was during one of these short naps that Garner and Sammy assisted Lizzie out to the car, together with a few supplies, then quietly drove away, leaving the safety of the house and the chamber behind.

Upon waking, the tall dark figure realised that he had missed the going of his quarry and he smashed items of furniture in a terrible rage.

But by then Garner had driven some miles Southwest and was now deep into the Surrey countryside.

Chapter 9

Garner drove carefully, aware that his patient, being cared for in the back of the car by Sammy, would probably appreciate fewer bumps and swerving as he steered in the direction of the north Kent countryside.

Apart from the usual array of abandoned vehicles the did not meet any sign of life until they turned off of a major motorway and began to cut through lanes in the beautiful rural county.

Garner had just driven downhill and around a right-hand bend when he was forced to swerve to avoid hitting a woman sitting in the centre of the road.

"What the f . . . . ?" he bit his tongue before the expletive could be heard.

Screeching to a halt, he put the vehicle in reverse and backed up alongside the figure who had not turned a hair at her near miss.

He wound the window down to speak to her.

But one look caused him to close the window quickly.

Filthy and dishevelled the woman sat as if in a trance, she held a bone that had some raw meat on it, and she was slowly tearing some of the meat with her teeth and chewing it.

Garner recoiled with horror.

For the limb that the woman was enjoying was a human arm that still had a tiny hand on the end, and by the size of it Garner decided that it was the arm of a very young child.

At first the woman seemed totally oblivious of Garner and the car.

Then she turned her face to look up at him.

Her ravaged features scared even the battle experienced ex-soldier, her dark circled eyes blazed insanely and she snarled animal-like at him with blackened and bloodied teeth.

Putting the car into first gear Garner pressed the accelerator and sped off, racing through the village that now came up fast, and completely forgetting his previous consideration for his sick passenger.

Fortunately neither Sammy or Lizzie had seen the putrid limb that the woman had and he said nothing to them, but stayed quiet when Lizzie questioned him on why he had stopped, then sped off like he had.

The nurse frowned and took on a puzzled expression.

As the car sped quickly through the village he saw, in the rear mirror, dozens of mad looking individuals coming out of the houses and shops and running after the car, waving and gesticulating wildly.

Since seeing for the first time how these people now looked and behaved, then there was no way that Garner was going to stop for them.

This was the first time that he had seen such a mob and he had no reason to stay near where such insane people could threaten him and his charges.

So he put his foot down on the accelerator and sped out of the area.

Soon they were miles from the village and once again in the quiet lanes of the countryside.

Garner slowed and, as it was becoming dark with heavy leaden rain clouds, he began to look for somewhere for them to stay safely overnight.

Then just up ahead, and some distance from the road, he saw a small farm and he turned up into a narrow lane and came to a halt outside the front door of the small farmhouse.

"Stay in the car. Do not leave it for any reason. Got it? Wait until I say so" he ordered.

Then leaving the girls in the car he entered the farmhouse and explored all of the rooms to determine how safe the building was.

The farmhouse was empty.

There was absolutely no sign of life at all.

He went out to the car and studied the immediate terrain.

He saw a filthy and neglected truck parked beside the dilapidated barn, but thought nothing of it.

And that was to prove to be a big mistake.

All was quiet and there was no movement anywhere.

He opened the car door and hastened the girls into the house, being particularly considerate with Lizzie as he helped her into the building and upstairs where he made her comfortable on a large double bed in a cosy bedroom.

"Are you hungry?" he asked her, and Lizzie, beginning to feel more comfortable with him replied, "Yes. I could do with a nice plate of steak and chips", she joked.

Garner grinned, "I'll see what I can do" he said and he went back downstairs.

Finding a few eggs in a cupboard he rustled up three omelettes on the small camping gas ring that he had brought along, after checking that the eggs were not bad.

Then he and Sammy ate ravenously before he took a plate full up to Lizzie.

He helped her sit up in the bed and he sat watching her as she too devoured it with relish.

"You *were* hungry, were'nt you" Garner smiled as he took the empty plate from her and left her to rest.

It had grown dark and was now raining heavily outside so Garner told Sammy to try and get some rest while he went back upstairs.

He helped Lizzie into a small bathroom where he started to change the dressing that he had put on her wound before they had left his house earlier that day.

There was no electricity so he had to work by the light of a couple of candles.

Lizzie sat hunched on the side of the bath as Garner cleaned the wound that was beginning to heal nicely.

Downstairs Sammy too had lit a candle and had pulled a blanket up over herself as she lay on an old worn settee when suddenly the door burst open and eight frightening figures rushed in, screaming insanely and making the youngster cringe in terror.

Garner heard the commotion downstairs and he attempted to leave the bathroom to protect his daughter but by the time he had moved to go downstairs, ordering Lizzie to "Stay there, and shut the door", the mad throng had left, carrying Sammy, screaming in her strange strangulated way, out into the black night.

Halfway down the stairs Garner looked out of a window to see the mob rushing over to the old truck that he had ignored earlier.

Some were carrying flaming torches and they appeared to be led by a wild spear-waving figure that looked like a nun in dirty black robes.

The figure turned and screamed at the building as if sensing that he was watching them.

She screamed dementedly and the torchlight caught her terribly scarred and ravaged features, a terrifying sight that made even Garner's blood run cold.

The face was so much like a Halloween mask, a horrific skeletal mask with deep black sunken eyes that glared with an insane fire, and with tight lips stretched over large snarling teeth.

Garner started to leave the farmhouse as the mob climbed aboard the truck and it drove off, careering wildly across the front of the farmhouse and smashing into the Volvo, forcing it up against the side of the house.

Garner had to dive for cover back into the farmhouse hallway as the truck swept close by, then it careered down the narrow lane and away from the farm.

He realised that he must follow but first he took stock of the situation, and rushing upstairs he told Lizzie that she must stay, locking herself in the upstairs bedroom, until he returned.

Hoping that would be the case he left the nurse and ran to the car.

It was wrecked.

The side and front of the Volvo was totally crushed and there was water and petrol running freely from underneath.

Cursing violently he ran back into the house to search for a weapon.

Searching deep within a cupboard in the hallway he found a shotgun and checking that there were cartridges for it he ran back out into the yard.

The Volvo had definitely had it.

Running over to the barn he discovered a tractor inside.

Garner jumped up on the seat and found that the farmer had left the ignition key in place.

He turned the key and the engine coughed a few times before noisily breaking into a healthy rumble.

Not the ideal vehicle for pursuing his quarry but it would have to do.

Putting the tractor into gear he drove it out of the barn and steered towards the lane that Sammy's abductors had sped down.

He refrained from putting on any lights as he considered that the mad group who had his daughter should not become aware of his attempt to follow them.

He drove as fast as he could, getting used to the awkward vehicle but almost turning it over as he raced around the narrow and very muddy bends.

Then, some distance ahead he spotted the truck.

It was still careering from side to side as if the driver had been drinking, heading towards an unlit row of houses and a public house, so he slowed to a halt some way back up the road.

The truck had stopped outside the pub and the occupants tumbled out and went inside.

Garner stayed on the tractor, his thoughts flashing and filling his mind as he considered his next move.

What should he do?

They had his precious Sammy.

And Lizzie was alone in the farmhouse some miles back.

Chapter 10

Sammy was terrified, and she had wet her knickers with fear.

A huge unkempt man who stunk horribly, making her retch dryly, held her tightly with one strong arm around her slim frame and a filthy hand clamped over her mouth.

She had struggled at first but to no avail and finally she had given up, exhausted by her efforts and now she cried chokingly, stifled by the filthy hand.

The lorry had sped along throwing the occupants in the back from side to side and the poor youngster was bruised as her body was crushed against the side of the lorry by the bulk of her unsympathetic captor.

Suddenly the lorry had screeched to a halt and the small group of dirty strangers had left the vehicle, and seemingly following the guttural orders of the figure dressed in the filthy black robes.

Sammy was part carried and part dragged into a public house where the man and one of the bedraggled women tied her wrists and ankles tightly with silken cord torn from the heavy drapes that framed the small windows.

All the time her captors drooled slick saliva freely over her, and she tore her eyes from their disfigured faces.

Sammy was then dumped roughly in the empty dark space of the inglenook fireplace.

The black robed figure continued to screech her orders, hitting out roughly at some of her followers.

Sammy cowered back into the darkness, her knees raised up in an attempt to make herself less visible and she watched with tears streaming down her face as the group began to lay around the bar area as if they had been told to rest and sleep.

She saw the leader take one of the younger men by the hand and drag him out of the bar, and she saw the man being led up some stairs until they were out of sight.

Very soon the sound of loud snoring filled the bar area as one by one the strange insane group fell asleep.

Sammy continued to sob behind the dirty cloth that the woman had wound tightly around her face, fearing for her life, and praying that God would help her.

And for her Daddy to come and rescue her.

What the hell was this?

And why her?

Sammy shivered and cried until her throat hurt.

Chapter 11

Garner had decided to reconnoitre the area immediately surrounding the small village Inn and he moved quickly from the tractor.

Discovering that the only sign of life was in the Inn he crept around the rear of the building to find a way to gain entrance and rescue his daughter.

A bright moonlight created a low light within what he made out to be the bar area and a few slowly moving shadows of dark figures preparing to sleep on the long bench seats, and some on the floor.

Then he made out black robed figure of the crazy leader.

She was gesticulating wildly and shrieking at two huge men who stood meekly and obeyed her.

Then the figure turned and swept away, going up some stairs in the far corner of the lounge, dragging a skinny youth by the hand.

The two men plodded over to the old inglenook fireplace where Garner now saw his daughter.

She had been tied up and had a wide piece of cloth wrapped around her face.

Sammy lay still inside the fireplace, her body curled up in the hearth.

He felt a sudden fear.

Was she dead?

If not then what did they intend to do with her?

But, and to Garner's relief, the two heavies sat down together beside the fireplace and leaning back against the wall they both closed their eyes and appeared to quickly fall into a deep sleep.

Now Garner made the decision to enter the building and use his expertise to rescue his daughter.

The back door to the Inn creaked as he slid inside but nobody seemed to hear and so he crept up to the door that led into the lounge bar area.

A figure was laying near the doorway on it's back with it's face turned upwards.

Garner recoiled at the sight of the man's face, then realised how badly it was ravaged by the disease.

Almost skeletal, the features were riven with long dark red and black sores, some were open abscesses, oozing sickly yellow pus.

The mouth was wide open and looked black inside where the few teeth that remained were jagged and badly coloured.

Taking a closer look Garner discovered that this man, one of those who he had seen running from the farmhouse, was actually now quite dead, his body already stiffening.

Garner crept across to where two figures lay toe to toe along a cushioned bench seat.

These two were alive and snorting pig-like snorts from their open mouths.

Although one of them was a female, and not too old at that, Garner swiftly rapped them both hard on their temples with the stock of the shotgun, rendering them completely unconscious.

Another figure lay under a table wrapped in a filthy blanket.

Garner silently disposed of this one and heard the skull crack as he again used the stock of the shotgun.

Now moving stealthily over to the two heavies he made to hit the nearest when the man roused from his slumber, saw him and began to get to his feet, snarling animal-like.

Garner slammed the shotgun's muzzle hard into the man's stomach then swung the weapon around to hit the man on the side of the head.

The man crashed back, falling across the stirring figure of his partner.

With a speed and a strength that Garner found quite surprising the remaining opponent easily threw his comrade aside and slashed at Garner with an evil looking blade.

Without any further consideration Garner raised the shotgun to waist height and fired one barrel directly into the man's stomach, throwing him backwards and into the fireplace where he fell on top of Sammy.

Garner threw down the weapon and knelt to pull the corpse off of her.

He helped Sammy to sit up and was untying her wrists when she suddenly looked up over his shoulders.

With horror in her eyes the youngster tried to warn her father, but a sudden hard blow hit him on the back of the head and he fell limply beside her.

An insane shriek filled the room and Sammy pushed herself further away, into the dark interior of the inglenook, an expression of sheer terror on her pretty face.

Chapter 12

Dawn was breaking as Garner regained consciousness.

Sammy was kneeling bt his side and bathing a nasty gash on the back of his head.

His head hurt like hell.

Like a steamroller had rolled across it.

Even his eyes felt swollen and aching.

He glanced around.

The gang who last night had abducted Sammy were very still, laying stiffly where he had left them, rigor mortis setting in.

He wondered who had hit him and why they had elected not to do him further harm and also as they were not obviously still around, why they had left him, and more importantly his daughter, without any further injury or even death.

What had been the point of Sammy's abduction?

"I need an Aspirin" he grunted, and he began to sit up.

"Whoa . . . ." he gasped and fell back, amazed at how weak he still was.

Sammy got to her feet and went over to the bar area where she poured a generous pouring of some brandy she found there and then returned to crouch down again beside her father.

He took it from her.

"Thanks, love" he said and managed a grateful smile before sipping the fiery liquid, then downing the remainder in one swallow.

Sammy continued to fuss over him and he allowed her to finish bathing his wound, clearing the matted blood from his short hair.

"Are you OK, love?" he asked his daughter, "Did they do anything . . . did they hurt you?"

Staring directly into her father's anxious face the youngster understood his concerns and she replied by hugging him and saying in her awkward garbled way, "OK . . . Mmmmm . . . O . . . OK . . ."

In her own peculiar way Sammy assured him that apart from the shock of being forcibly taken, they had not harmed her in any way, just terrorised her that was all.

She then, by using hand signs and her tortuous garble managed to tell her father of the strange reaction of the woman in the dirty black robes.

Apparently the woman had suddenly reeled back after seeing Sammy full face for the first time, and upon kneeling and studying Garner's features she had risen and waving her arms around and wailing dementedly she had fled the building, running out into the dark night and the torrential rain.

It all made no sense to Garner.

Perhaps the mad ravings of a poor insane creature shocked by the events of the night.

Who could say?

He struggled, and with his daughter's help, he got to his feet.

"We had better get out of here" he said, "She may come back with more of these poor ungodly creatures".

"Let's go", and picking up the shotgun he led Sammy from the building.

He was afraid that being in the close proximity of the diseased corpses could put his daughter in danger, although she had been held close to sick victims of the virus last night.

For to his knowledge the youngster had been entirely free of any contact or symptoms of the deadly virus before this.

On edge and prepared for any sly attack he took Sammy away from the village and by the time that they reached the tractor he was feeling a little better.

Climbing up on to the seat of the tractor he lifted Sammy up and held her on his lap then drove carefully back to the farm.

It was very quiet at the farm and Garner was worried for Lizzie, but was very relieved to find her, still upstairs where he had told her to stay, with a chair rammed up against the door handle.

It had taken some loud knocking on the door to wake Lizzie from the deep sleep that she was in.

But she was very relieved upon hearing Garner's voice calling her, and she just managed to get the door open before he prepared to shoulder charge it.

The nurse still appeared weak and exhausted but was a little better than the day before.

Garner covered her with a blanket then went downstairs.

"Let's find some grub" Garner suggested and he and Sammy searched the large kitchen and the old barn, eventually finding fresh eggs which he cooked on the small mobile gas ring together with the contents of a tin of corned beef.

Sammy heated up some water and they had a brew of tea made with tea bags.

They were eating quietly when Lizzie appeared, bleary eyed.

"Mmmm, something smells good", she said, licking her lips.

She had smelt the food cooking and had discovered that she was quite ravenous.

So Sammy left her seat at the table and soon rustled up a similar dish of food for her new friend.

Later, and feeling somewhat better for eating some food, they sat at the kitchen table and Garner told the nurse of the previous night's events.

Lizzie listened intently and when he got to the part of the story where he had been struck on the head she got up to examine the wound.

"Mmmm, nasty, but you'll live", she said with a chuckle, and this surprised Garner, for it was the first time that she had shown any personal feelings since her own 'incident'.

"You're getting better". Garner winced as she pressed a clean plaster from their kit on to the wound.

Now he became serious.

"We must still try to get to a place of safety. A place where there is some civilised control, and some authority exists", he told the girls.

"And I know of a place where that might be", he mused, obviously thinking hard on a distant memory.

He had mentioned it to them before and now he elucidated.

He told them of the military establishment he knew of from his SAS days, deep in the Dorset countryside, where they might find the sort of organisation that he talked about.

"We'll make for there. It could be dangerous with all of these loonies out there but we must try" he told them.

He laid out a route that he planned to take, using an old road atlas of Southern England.

"But first we need good transport. We cannot go all the way on a tractor" he said.

So he organised the girls to pack some essentials.

Garner found that he was pleasantly surprised to find that his daughter and Lizzie had become close and the youngster had taken it upon herself to care for the wounded nurse.

He found a couple of rucksacks and they proceeded to fill them with food.

Tins of corned beef, beans, etc., and what was left of the good bread and eggs that they had discovered in the farmhouse.

He also packed some salt, and filled two empty plastic containers with water that he previously boiled to ensure that it was safe.

Next he rolled up three heavy blankets from the bedroom, and found some wet weather clothing in the cupboard under the stairs.

Various other items went into the rucksacks.

Three torches, spare batteries, and matches, although he still had his cigarette lighter in his pocket.

Garner had in fact given up smoking months before, but held on to his old favourite lighter.

Finally he took the double-barrelled shotgun that he used at the inn together with a supply of cartridges.

Feeling ready despite his aching head, and Lizzie's weakness, he led the girls away from the farm.

It was late morning and the weather had become very humid and the boggy ground hindered their progress.

He allowed the girl's a few short rests but finally decided that he had to get transport soon.

So leaving them sitting under a thickly leafed shrub with the packs, Garner scouted ahead and silently reconnoitred the small hamlet where last night's events had taken place.

There was absolutely no living person around, only the putrid decomposing bodies that were still laying around.

Then behind a very well kept bungalow he discovered a Range Rover that looked in good condition.

Smashing the glass of the back door he was able to gain entry into the kitchen area and there on the worktop, together with a man's wallet and gloves, Garner found some car keys.

Taking just the keys Garner found that they fitted the Range Rover and he climbed in and started the engine.

The car roared into life and he felt the raw slick power under his control, and he immediately felt more confident of their chances.

Racing back to where he had left the two girls Garner quickly got them aboard and turned again in the direction he had planned to take towards their goal.

As he drove speedily but with care through the small hamlet and out into the countryside again he failed to see a small sports car some distance behind and just creep into view.

The sports car driver put down the binoculars on the seat beside his and smiled, reaching for his lighter to light a cheroot that he held between his thin lips.

"So. That's where you got to" the man grinned as he puffed away on the cheroot, "Well, me old mate, I'm going to be watching you from now on" and he patted the sniper's rifle

John Veary

that lay on the passenger seat and he drove easily, keeping Garner's vehicle just in his sight ahead of him.

Garner, oblivious of their shadow some distance behind, got Lizzie to open the road map booklet, to the page showing their route, and said, "Right. Let's see what happens next. Blandford Forum here we come".

Chapter 13

They had eaten as much as they could before they left the farm.

Garner did not know when they might be in a position to eat comfortably next.

It was late afternoon and the girls, particularly Lizzie, were feeling very tired so Garner decided to stop somewhere for the night.

Driving along the road hr had spotted a new looking building that turned out to be a barn, beside the road, so he pulled in and they went into the refurbished building and made themselves comfortable.

Garner drove the car around behind the barn and out of sight of the road.

He scouted around the immediate area to check that all was well before he too settled down for the night in the barn.

Both girls were already sleeping.

Sitting near the barn door he rested against the wall and dozed.

A mix of dreams troubled his slumber, causing him to moan and toss his head a little until he eventually slid into a deep sleep.

The night passed uneventfully and they awoke at dawn to eat a small breakfast of biscuits and long-life milk.

It was a chilly morning and so they wrapped themselves up in extra clothing that they had discovered in the back of the Range Rover.

Then feeling refreshed and ready for their journey they started off, their destination Blandford Forum.

Driving at a steady pace, and passing through small villages that showed no sign of life, they eventually arrived at Blandford Forum.

It was early afternoon.

Lizzie had been feeling much better and she had relaxed and had slept during the journey.

It had started to rain heavily as they entered the outskirts of the town so Garner pulled into the large car park of a giant superstore.

The rain drummed noisily on the roof of the Range Rover so they sat quietly for a while waiting for it to abate before alighting from the vehicle.

They had no reason to hurry, but obviously a real reason to be very careful and aware of the possible dangers from any of the infected people that might be around.

After thirty minutes or so the rain began to lessen and their view of the surroundings became clearer.

Suddenly Sammy sat up and motioned with one hand, making her peculiar noises, to get their attention.

They saw a person making his way along the side of the store, seemingly feeling his way as if he was having a problem with his sight.

The person, a youth, staggered awkwardly into the main entrance and disappeared inside.

Quietly, leaving the girls in the car, Garner walked across the car park and silently entered the store behind the unsuspecting youth.

He found the lad searching for tinned food, grappling clumsily with both hands, and quietly crying with frustration.

It was obvious to Garner that the lad was blind.

He purposefully rattled a box of cereals to let the lad know that he was near.

The lad froze.

"It's OK, lad" Garner said, and he approached the youth, talking to him to reassure him that he was a friend.

At first the youth was very frightened and suspicious of Garner but gradually he relaxed and he felt safe, and the feeling of Garner's arm about his shoulders prompted the youth to sob.

Garner took the lad by the hand and he led him from the store and back to the Range Rover.

The youth, upon hearing the voice of Lizzie, and the strange guttural noises of Sammy, began to feel better and he was invited into the warmth of the car and he sat between the girls.

The newcomer told them that his name was Tom.

Tom Leonard.

He was just nineteen years of age.

"I became ill with the 'flu' a few weeks ago" he told them, "Bad it was. Me mother called a friend with a car and I ended up in St. Mary's Hospital. Me fever was really bad."

Tom could not remember how long he had been in hospital but after getting over the fever he found that he had lost his sight.

"I'm not totally blind, you know, It's like everything is white and with black things moving when I try to focus".

Tom paused, obviously emotional at his new weakness.

"I can just about see blurred images, but otherwise I'm blind". He began to sob again.

After a moment he calmed himself and continued to tell them of his misfortunes.

Someone had assisted him with his clothes and had ushered him out into the night and he had discovered that no one seemed to be around.

"No traffic. No sign of life at all. It was weird", he said.

"Except . . . ." And he paused, " . . . during the second night I sat in a bus shelter, at least I think it was a bus shelter, and I heard this horrible screaming coming nearer.

I got down, under the bus shelter seat and rolled myself up into a ball. I was terrified".

Tom told them that he stumbled on the superstore after living rough in an old van parked on the perimeter of the car park.

"I found my way into the store and got hold of some tinned stuff. I was lucky, I found the rack where things, like kitchen bits and bobs were, and felt for and got a tin opener, so I managed to eat from the tins. You know, beans and spaghetti, sausages too. All the fresh veggies were rotten. Some of the apples and pears were OK though".

He went on, "And the meat counters were horrible. All of the meat had gone off and stunk to high heaven".

Tom managed a tearful grin when he realised how adept he had actually become, using his sense of smell to determine what was edible and safe.

He choked back tears when he told them that his father had died earlier and that he had been told whilst in hospital that his mother was seriously ill.

"I believe that she has died as well" he said quietly.

Sammy wrinkled her nose at the stale smell emitting from Tom and Lizzie suggested that they find somewhere for them all to clean up.

"We could do with a good bath, if that is at all possible" she said, winking at Sammy.

"Firstly we are going to stock up a bit, and this is the ideal place to do it" Garner said, then "C'mon Tom, come with me. Let's get some supplies from good old Sainsburys"

Garner led Tom back into the store where the youth stood by a trolley and loaded it with the various items, mainly tinned food, that Garner passed to him.

Then after taking the 'stolen' or 'borrowed' goods back to the car, they moved off into the town where they discovered an up-market hotel near the end of the main street.

Parking the Range Rover round the back of the hotel in the private car park, and where there were just three other vehicles, they made their way into the hotel via the tradesmen's entrance, bringing some of their recently acquired supplies with them.

Absolutely no one else had been seen during their drive to the hotel or now, within the building.

Garner got them to take two rooms on the first floor, one for the girls, and one for him and Tom.

A bath of cold water was prepared in the room shared by the men and Garner told Tom to get in it and scrub himself clean, giving him some soap and body talc for afterwards.

The youth did so and Garner rummaged around in other rooms and found the lad some clean and more pleasant smelling clothing.

Garner then bathed himself in a bath full of clean but very cold water and he felt much better for being cleaner after he had dried himself and dressed in fresh clothing he had found in the hotel.

He had noticed a ladies' clothiers across the street so with eyes darting about the area he went over to the shop and helped himself to a variety of clothing, including a bag full of mixed underwear, and other strong practical items of clothing for Lizzie and Sammy.

He did know of their sizes so he took a wide range of clothing.

Lizzie and Sammy had also bathed and were wearing warm towelling robes supplied by the hotel.

Lizzie sorted the clothing Garner had shyly handed them before he quickly withdrew from their room.

Lizzie found items of underwear and clothing to suit her, and of good sizes, and she felt so much better now that she was clean and smelling sweetly with some expensive perfume that she and Sammy had discovered in their bathroom.

Her wound felt good as Sammy had applied a fresh clean dressing for her.

There was no clothing that really fitted the youngster but just for a laugh she donned some of the outsize items that her father had brought over.

And she went along to the 'boys' room and posed in the oversize gear making Garner laughed loudly.

He explained to Tom the reason for his outburst and the lad grinned happily.

Eventually Lizzie sorted some male clothing that she found in an adjoining room and this fitted the youngster who smiled cheekily as once again she showed her father her new boyish image.

Going down to the kitchen they warmed some tinned food on the portable gas ring that Lizzie had found in one of the large cupboards. There was also a box of unused gas canisters which they also purloined.

Then after dining in the sumptuous hotel dining room, using the best silver, they retired for the night, although Garner stayed for a while, helping himself to a couple of glasses of fine malt whisky from the bar.

It was during the night that Sammy rushed in to wake her father, and due to the drink and tiredness, she had to shake him roughly to bring him to a state of consciousness.

Garner had lain on top of the bed and was still fully clothed.

Tom woke upon hearing the commotion of Sammy's frantic guttural sounds and he followed them, his hands feeling along the walls, as Sammy dragged her father by the hand out of the room and over the hallway to a bedroom opposite theirs where Lizzie was watching from the side of a tall window.

The nurse put a finger to her lips in a silent gesture for them to make no sound.

"There's some movement over there. See? The other side of the Baker's shop" she whispered.

Garner crept over and stood beside her.

He slowly eased the heavy curtain aside and looked out over the front area of the hotel.

It appeared that Lizzie had become restless and had got up and decided to roam the hotel floor upon which they were staying.

She had wandered into this room and something had made her look out of the window.

It was a bright moonlit night with just a few small scudding clouds.

And what she saw had prompted her to go to Sammy and tell her to get Garner.

At first he saw nothing, then Lizzie whispered, "here . . . ." and she pointed.

Garner watched as two people, a man and a woman, moved slowly and furtively from shop doorway to shop doorway along the parade of shops that faced the hotel.

Then, just as the couple were in between two shop doorways, and moving together holding hands, two shots rang out one after the other, and both of them fell still to the pavement, black blood running freely from head wounds.

Garner knew from the sound of the shots that a high powered weapon had just been used, and that the unfortunate couple were almost definitely dead.

Neither of the prostrate bodies moved, and the pools of blood now surrounded their heads.

Quietly signalling that the others stay quiet, he took the shotgun and crept out from the rear of the hotel.

Moving expertly he approached the area from which he was certain the shots had originated.

Stealthily Garner crept into a dark alleyway, listening intently for any sounds and his eyes flitting everywhere.

Checking that it was safe he moved further into the alley.

The moonlight glinted on two bright metal items on the ground.

He stooped and studied them before picking them up.

This confirmed his suspicions.

He held two brass bullet cases of a calibre that meant it had been a high powered rifle, a sniper's rifle.

It had been from here that the killer had slain his unknowing prey.

Squinting in the darkness around the ground area Garner found some fresh stubs of an unusual cheroot that the killer had enjoyed whilst stalking his victims.

The cheroots reminded him of an old comrade who had become an adversary.

Garner shuddered, a strange feeling coming over him.

Then making quite certain that there was no longer any threat, and that took him over an hour, and after checking that the recent victims were indeed very dead both with a single bullet wound to the back of the head he crept back to the hotel where he told the others to go back to their rooms and try to sleep.

It was only then that Garner sat in a chair at the end of the corridor, gun by his side, and kept watch for the remainder of the night, his mind buzzing, perplexed by the strange and evil act that they had witnessed earlier.

Garner eventually fell into a deep and nightmarish slumber.

Chapter 14

Garner allowed the others to sleep late the following morning, keeping himself alert until 9.30am then he quietly went around waking each of them and advising them to go quietly down to the hotel kitchen and feed themselves.

He then lay on top of one of the large beds in one of the most expensive suites and fell asleep.

His years of army life and the harsh training he had experienced in the SAS meant that he awoke after an hour, almost as if he had an inner alarm clock.

A wash in cold water refreshed him and he joined the others.

They began to pack up various items that he told them might be needed, and all except Tom searched the service areas and the kitchen enthusiastically, finding some items that Garner advised as useful, and others that were not in least any good at all.

They piled their goods, including a supply of sheets and blankets, even pillows, into the back of a brand new Mercedes 4 x 4 that Garner had his eye on.

He had discovered the keys in the hotel reception with a name tag "Mr. Curtis—Manager", and had decided, after checking it's fuel situation, that he would take it in place of the Range Rover.

So with the car packed, including the spare cane of fuel that they had brought with them in the Range Rover, they left the hotel around midday.

Both girls said that they felt a little sad at leaving the comfort of the hotel.

Garner had studied paths and the road, taking some time to determine that they were under no obvious threat, particularly from the mystery gunman.

So making themselves comfortable in the new vehicle the girls watched as Garner started the engine, it's soft purring giving them all a sense of confidence in the next lap of their journey.

It felt good and Garner steered out of the car park, then out along the road leading out of town.

Mr. Curtis would not be missing his new car.

Garner was sure of that.

Once clear of town he put his foot down on the accelerator and they sped out into the lush green countryside.

Soon he was driving at over seventy miles per hour, feeling quite content and in full control of the car.

No other vehicle was sighted as they moved across the country and as they travelled he again repeated the plan to get to the secret army camp that he knew of deep in the rolling hills of Dorset, not too far from the army training area used by tanks.

He told them again that he hoped to find members of the military there and would join them, ensuring a safe haven for all of them.

They had just rounded a bend on a downward slope when Tom, who had been requesting a 'wee' stop, suddenly insisted that he could wait no longer and "needed to go now!"

Pulling over, into a lay-by beside a grassy bank, Garner allowed them all to get out and stretch their legs, and saw Tom turn away to relieve himself in the road.

A high wooden fence was erected the length of the road here and as far as the eye could see.

But just adjacent to where they were parked there was a break in the fence.

Strong winds or something else had caused one of the wooden panels to come free of a fencepost and was leaning inwards at one end, creating a gap.

They heard the sharp yapping of a small dog and Sammy had looked through the gap in the fence where she saw a small white "Scottie" dog running along what had once been a railway line, and into a tunnel.

The little dog reappeared, ran a short distance towards them, stopped and gave them a few more shrill yaps, and then it turned and ran back into the tunnel again.

It was if it was inviting them to follow it.

Sammy pleaded with her father in her own inimitable way to go after the animal and Garner relented.

"Stay in the car" he told Lizzie, "And Tom. Wait for us to return. Keep down should you hear of any other cars coming. OK?"

Although the beautiful surroundings appeared peaceful and serene he took the shotgun with him, always aware of a possible attack from the sick and crazy people.

The railway track and sleepers had long gone and now tall grass and weeds marked the line of the old track that led to a set of iron gates, padlocked in the centre, that barred entry into the tunnel.

Garner could hear the dog still yapping and so he forced the rusting padlock open with a piece of steel rod conveniently discovered nearby, and he and his daughter went into the dark interior of the tunnel.

The now distant yapping of the dog could just about be heard.

Sammy looked worriedly at her father.

He smiled at her, "Don't worry, love. I reckon the little fella wants us to follow him".

Garner did not know why he said that but somehow he felt that it was plausible.

Looking deep into the darkness they could see no light in the distance at all so Sammy was sent back quickly to the 4 x 4 to fetch a couple of torches.

They were about to enter the tunnel when Lizzie and Tom came behind them.

Garner shrugged his broad shoulders when Lizzie said that she felt that they should stick together, so they all now began to walk into the dark depths listening for the dog's faraway barking.

They followed the torch beams along where the old rail track once curved, and they now lost sight of their entry point and it became pitch black.

Lizzie was holding Tom by the hand and leading him as they followed Sammy and Garner.

"Ooooo . . . it's so dark in here" Lizzie shuddered, "I don't like it".

Tom squeezed her hand, "Don't be afraid. I'm sure it's alright" he said.

Garner was swinging his torch from side to side, trying to pin-point the direction from where the dog was barking.

They came upon an arched doorway, brick built by the Victorians, that was once used by railway men as a safe point, should they be working or inspecting the inside of the tunnel in the days when trains passed through here.

There was a step up to the archway.

The archway appeared to be about three feet in depth.

Garner stepped up on to the narrow walkway that led into the recess and putting a finger to his lips and shining his torch up into his face he signalled to the others to keep quiet.

Lizzie whispered in Tom's ear, "Shhh . . . don't speak or make any sound, Ron needs quietness for a moment".

They could still hear the faint sounds of the little dog yapping, and it appeared to be coming from within the archway.

Garner crouched and lowered the beam of his torch discovering that the brick wall was the rear face of the archway and it had a few bricks missing at the base.

Garner whistled.

"Here . . . here, boy . . . here . . . c'mon . . . ." he called.

The sharp yapping stopped momentarily then began again, seemingly closer then becoming faint again, as if the animal had heard them, and then had come closer to call them before continuing on it's way, maybe trying to lead them somewhere . . . . or to someone?

Garner told the others to stand back and he kicked hard at the lower bricks where the hole seemed weakest and after a few hefty blows with his strong steel-capped boots almost all of the back wall gave way and collapsed creating a great billow of sooty dust, and a rush of warmer air met them.

As the dust settled they crowded forward to look along a narrow tunnel that appeared to run for a great distance in a straight line and graduating upwards.

There was no dampness, just dry dusty air, and a hint of light in the far distance.

Garner led them along the narrow tunnel and he had to bend his upper body as it was only about five feet six inches to roof height.

Obviously, when the tunnel was built, people were generally shorter in height.

The height did not bother the girls, or Tom, who were all shorter.

It took them about fifteen minutes before they found themselves approaching a small square cell that had daylight originating from a higher position.

The cell was constructed in large blocks of Limestone and there was a short flight of steps that led upwards to a partially open heavy wooden door.

They followed Garner up the steps and he peered around the door to find that it was in the back of a large and wide recess that was part of the side of a huge hallway.

He noticed that the reverse of the door was disguised as panelling and from the hallway side of the door it did not look like a door at all.

A secret door, perhaps?

Taking in the whole surroundings it became apparent that they were inside the hallway of a large country house.

Many of these old houses had secret doors and passages, built in the far off days of the English Civil war as secret escape routes.

Garner signalled for the others to follow him quietly and stay silent as they emerged from the dark cell and into the large main hall of the building.

It was very quiet and even the dog could not be heard as they stood looking around the vast hallway.

They had found themselves inside a Georgian Mansion, with many doors leading off on either side of the hallway, and two main heavy carved doors were to their left that were the entrance doors.

To their left were two wide curved staircases that swept up from each side of the hallway and met on the first floor leading to a long and wide landing.

"Hello! Is anyone there?" Garner called out suddenly, causing the others to jump nervously.

At first there was no response, then Tom who had remarkable hearing, hushed them and they listened hard.

"There . . . . hear him?" Tom cried out, "Up there" and he pointed up the great stairway.

They heard the faint plaintive cries now, somewhere up on the first floor and seemingly at some distance.

"OK" Garner said, "You three stay here. I'll see what's going on" and he started up the stairs.

As a precaution he held the shotgun in readiness.

Arriving at the wide expansive landing area he started off down a corridor from where he could make out the weak cries of an elderly man.

"Here . . . Please . . . in here . . . ." The voice came from a room on Garner's left.

He stood beside the open door and peered cautiously into the room.

The man was laying on a huge four-poster bed, against a pile of huge pillows that appeared stained, and with bundles of heavy looking sheets and blankets topped with a great quilt spread over him.

He was surrounded by empty packets of food and tins that were open and beginning to smell.

The man was obviously very ill and appeared to Garner that he was near to death.

But he had no signs of the virus, the black blotches and bright red blemishes.

He appeared to be very old.

Garner thought that the man was about eighty years old, or more, it was difficult to estimate due to the yellow pallor of his shrunken features.

The thin parchment skin stretched over the bony cheeks and chin.

The old man looked relieved but in pain as Garner went over to the bedside.

The Scottie dog now lay on the bed with it's mouth agape, it's tongue out and panting as if it too was on the way out.

But the small animal had achieved it's purpose by bringing help.

Going over to the doorway Garner called the others up.

"Who are you? Are you from the Government?" the old man asked Garner, his voice rasping as he gasped for breath.

Lizzie entered the room leaving Sammy holding Tom by the hand at the door.

The nurse went immediately over to the old man and felt his forehead, then took his pulse.

The man looked up at with rheumy eyes and a puzzled expression on his wizened face.

"Are you a medical person?" he enquired.

"Yes. I'm a nurse. How long have you been ill, and on your own?" she replied.

"Oh, I've been on my own for a few weeks now, since my brother died, and I have cancer and have been getting worse for two months I think" the man told her.

He glanced from Lizzie to Garner and back again.

"My name is Robert Cecil Durran, and I am the brother of the late Squire who died a few weeks ago. I suppose you might say that I am now the new Squire". And he smiled an ironic smile.

It appeared that Robert was the only survivor since the virus had wiped out every member of his family and their staff.

He continued, his voice halting at times as he struggled for breath.

"My brother. Angus. He . . . he . . . ." Robert ran out of breath and his head fell back on to the pillow.

Lizzie looked across at Garner and shook her head.

"Take it easy, fella" Garner said and he sat on the bed opposite to where Lizzie crouched over the old man.

Robert momentarily closed his eyes, and then he continued with his story.

"When I realised that I was the only one left, and that my damned cancer was winning, I decided to come to bed".

He paused again, breathing harshly.

It was obvious that it was very difficult for him to speak for long minutes.

"I have something very important to pass on, you see. And I thought that I might last out long enough to tell someone like you. It is so very important".

He looked seriously and directly at Garner.

"I realised that I must rest and try to fight this damn disease so I stocked myself up with plenty of foodstuffs and water, and of course my favourite Malt" and he motioned his head to the half full bottle of Malt Whisky beside the bed.

"I am aware of those damn crazy people roaming about. Some of them came here a couple of nights ago. Came up here. I pretended to be dead" he laughed and paused again to gasp for breath, "That bit was easy".

Robert now looked down at where the dog lay at his feet.

"Oh yes. And old Dougal. He has been my very good friend. I believe that maybe he is even responsible for bringing you to me, Eh?"

"How long have you been stuck here in this bed?" Lizzie asked.

Robert screwed up his eyes and seemed to consider his answer.

"A little over two weeks. I'm not utterly sure" he said quietly, "Time seems to have no meaning anymore, does it?"

Lizzie had been spending these last few minutes cleaning the old gentleman up, then prompted by Garner she took Sammy and Tom downstairs, looking for the kitchen where they were to prepare something to eat.

The kitchen was vast and had a huge fireplace, which Lizzie with Tom's help, laid quickly and got a fire going.

Then after tending to old Robert she spent some minutes thoroughly scrubbing her hands.

Stored neatly about the fireplace she noticed a plentiful array of cooking utensils that had once serviced a large household.

Gathering as many pots as she could manage, some hanging from the large cast-iron hooks over the fireplace, Lizzie filled them with water from a tap beside the large Belfast sink, then she re-hung them over the now roaring fire.

Some of the hot water would enable them to clean themselves properly later, she thought.

But meanwhile tea and coffee was the order of the day, then the warming up of some tins of soup that they had discovered in the huge kitchen pantry.

Dougal the Scottie dog had followed them down after getting a smell of warming soup, and having taken to Tom he sat on the lad's lap watching as Sammy and Lizzie prepared dishes for their supper.

Upstairs the old gentleman was feeling a little more comfortable since Lizzie had cleaned him up, and he began again to tell Garner more of his 'secrets'.

He reached beneath a pillow beside his head and with a shaking hand he held out a Browning automatic hand-gun to Garner.

"Here . . . take it . . . it's no good to me" he gasped.

Garner took it and he checked the weapon.

It was well maintained and had a full clip of ammunition.

Robert's voice had grown weaker and Garner had to lean closer to hear the old man.

"My brother, Angus, had been an active member of the scientist group working for the government".

Wheezing now from the exertion of continuously talking, Robert went on, "He was an eminent scientist himself, revered throughout the world. Known for his work in the field of new strains of influenza and associated infections".

The voice was now even weaker.

"Rest . . . take it easy . . ." Garner tried to advise the old man, but he shook his head, intent on telling Garner all that he could.

"Angus had become quite excited just days before he became ill" Robert continued.

"He told me that he had locked in to an answer to this vile epidemic and had probably discovered the beginnings of an antidote, if that's what you call it".

Robert closed his eyes, his breathing becoming more urgent.

"Papers. Get the papers!" he rasped huskily.

"Papers? What papers?" Garner asked, leaning even closer to Robert's face to hear the faint words.

Robert pointed at the door.

"Downstairs. In the study . . . .". And he squeezed his eyes shut as if a sudden pain had shuddered through his thin body, and he coughed violently, bloodied spittle on his bottom lip.

He quietened down and managed to continue, "There's a large painting . . . . over the fireplace . . . ."

Another cough racked his body, a deep gurgling cough.

With is eyes closed and an expression of pure pain on his face old Robert managed more information, "The safe . . . papers are in there . . . get them . . . get them . . . to . . . authority . . . somewhere . . . .".

Garner knew just how near to death old Robert was now.

"How do I get into the safe?" he asked the old man, "Is there a key, or a combination, perhaps?"

Garner felt Robert's cold clammy hand grip his.

"Here . . . it's here . . . my hand . . . ." He rasped.

Garner took the hand and studied it, finding nothing on the back of it.

He turned the hand over and spread the claw-like fingers, opening the palm.

And there, written in biro in the centre of Robert's palm was a six digit number.

Garner found Robert's biro on the bedside table and he wrote this number on the back of his own hand.

"Do try . . . to get . . . the papers . . . Angus's work . . . to the . . . the . . . .". Robert said no more.

Garner studied the old man's face.

Robert's eyes were wide open, his mouth slack, and Garner knew that the old man had just died.

Checking, Garner took the thin wrist and felt for a pulse.

None. Old Robert had finally found rest, and fortunately he had passed on information that he had felt a duty to.

Garner checked for any pulse on Robert's throat as well before pulling a sheet up to cover the old man's face.

He stood up and bowing his head in respect Garner walked over to a window and looked out into the darkening night.

Now he had another reason to successfully reach his goal.

Wrapped in his thoughts, worrying on how to make sure that he could satisfy old Robert's request and his own resolve with his daughter, together now with Lizzie and Tom, he was blinded to movement outside that normally he would have spotted.

Downstairs the three were beginning to rest, the warmth of the fire making them feel quite tired.

It was dark outside now.

Suddenly Dougal leapt from Tom's lap and ran over to a window, yapping and snarling fiercely.

Garner heard a commotion downstairs and the sound of splintering wood and breaking glass.

With the newly acquired weapon in his hand Garner raced out of the room and was running down the stairs when he saw five intruders about to enter the kitchen.

They appeared to be like the mob at the inn two nights previous, living but with the strange insanity brought on by the epidemic.

One was already attacking young Tom, who although blind was aware of the imminent danger, and he fell against his assailant and they rolled on the floor, punching and scratching at each other.

Toms flailing feet swept across the fire.

He felt the heat and he drew his legs away, dragging some of the glowering embers across the rug that lay before the fireplace.

In the fray nobody noticed at first that the embers had caught the rug alight and this reached to a hanging table cloth on the table.

Sammy jumped on the man who was now on top of Tom and she pulled the man's long lank hair and covered his eyes with her fingertips, digging them into his eyeballs.

The man screamed, a piercing scream, his mouth opening wide to reveal the black bloody and pointed teeth.

Lizzie meanwhile had picked up a pot of boiling water from the hook hanging over the fire and she threw the contents directly into the faces of two of the attackers.

They both screamed in agony and clawed at their faces with filthy hands.

The two remaining intruders turned and rushed out of the room, one of them armed with a vicious looking knife and the other carried a pitchfork.

They ran into Garner as he reached the hallway and before they could attack him he coldly shot both of them in the head.

Rushing headlong into the kitchen Garner saw Tom's attacker about to bring a poker down on the lad's head, although he still had Sammy on his back.

Garner ran over and he shoved the man sideways.

Sammy rolled away.

Cooly, and quite coldly, Garner aimed deliberately and shot the man between the eyes.

One of the screaming men, his face boiling with the water that Lizzie had thrown over him, tottered unsteadily towards her.

Lizzie picked up a broom and pushed him away causing him to fall backwards into the roaring fire.

The man screamed in a terrible agony before succumbing to the pain and dying, his clothing catching fire and his body fat beginning to sizzle.

The last of the attackers, backing away from Lizzie, and holding his hands over his scorched eyes, blubbering and sobbing, fell over the prone body of Sammy and hit his head on the corner of the table.

Garner checked him for any sign of life.

"He's dead" was all that he said before checking around for any other intruders.

Then he gathered the girls and Tom together.

He looked purposefully at each of them, "You all OK?" he asked them.

Breathless but very frightened they shook their heads.

Yes! They were OK!

The fire had really caught a hold on the kitchen furniture by now.

The old wood, dry for so many years, burnt fiercely and they were forced out into the hallway.

"Make for the tunnel . . . ." Garner ordered.

"What? Where are you going?" Lizzie shouted above the roar of the intense fire.

"Go . . . do as I say . . . I won't be long . . . have to get something" Garner managed to call back to her as he left them to find the study.

"What about the old gentleman?" Lizzie called after him as he raced away.

Calling back over his shoulder Garner said briefly, "He's dead".

The blaze had spread rapidly and Garner felt the heat even as ran into the study.

There. He saw the portrait over the fireplace and he strode over to it and tore the painting from the wall.

The safe was revealed now and Garner quickly punched in the numbers written on his hand.

The safe now opened and he grabbed every bit of paper and packages that were in it, and he stuffed everything into his pockets as he ran back out into the hallway and then down the steps into the tunnel.

The fire roared behind him and the heat was unbearable.

Squires Manor was to be a blackened shell the following morning.

Moving quickly Garner ushered his small party into a run and they made their way urgently out into the cool of the dark night, finding their 4 x 4 untouched and just where they had left it.

Sitting inside the vehicle, panting from their flight, they realised that they had an addition to their ranks . . . .

Dougal.

Garner grinned.

He did not mind at all!

After all it had been the little dog that had warned them of the attack, and they may have all been seriously harmed, even killed, if it had not been for him.

"Right" Garner finally said, "I think that we have had enough excitement for one day, don't you?"

And starting the engine he pulled away, again driving westwards in the direction that he felt safety lay.

And so, in the darkness, they travelled steadily, Tom and the girls sleeping, completely unaware that some distance behind them a sports car trailed them, it's lights extinguished, it's driver grinning evilly.

Chapter 15

Garner had taken a wrong turn in the dark and had found himself heading for the pretty coastal village of Lulworth Cove, where he decided to take a days rest provided it was going to be safe enough to do so.

There is only the one road that leads down to the little bay and he drove slowly and carefully down this road, his eyes searching for any threat or any sign of life.

The small hamlet appeared to be deserted, so he drew up and parked near the end of the road in front of a two storey building that had been a bed and breakfast business.

"Stay in the car" he ordered the others, "Lock yourselves in. I'm just going to scout around".

"Going to see if it's safe . . . ." He continued, and then he left the vehicle and disappeared into the darkness.

He had turned off the cars lights before he left and the girls and Tom now sat quietly in the snug warmth of the vehicle, not speaking but waiting anxiously for him to return.

Sammy fidgeted and Lizzie heard the youngster groaning, her strange gurgling sounds somewhat worrying.

"What's the matter, love?" Lizzie whispered in the darkness.

"Dddaaadd . . . lllnnggg . . . tiiimmme" Lizzie heard Sammy's difficult attempt to speak.

"Yes, he is. But he needs to be sure that everything is OK before we get out" Lizzie reassured the worried youngster.

Their eyes had become accustomed to the darkness now and Lizzie noticed that Tom was holding Sammy's hand as he sat beside her.

Lizzie smiled.

She had noticed how the couple had somehow been communicating with each other despite their separate physical problems.

A dark shadow suddenly reared up beside the vehicle making Sammy squeak out loudly with fear.

A face appeared at the window on the driver's side.

It was Garner.

He signalled for Lizzie to release the car's locking system and open the door.

She did and he climbed in.

"Right. Everything seems to be safe. I've checked the buildings on both sides of the road, right up to where the field begin. Not a soul about. Not even dead ones" he told them, "The whole village is deserted".

"So, gather all of our gear, all of the bags that we packed in the hotel in Blandford, and we're going to stay a while in this B&B" and he pointed at the house outside which they had parked.

He had discovered that the B&B had looked very inviting inside and was the ideal place for them to rest.

Garner led them into the building, making sure that the 4 x 4 was secure, and also the doors of the B&B were locked after they had settled down inside.

He ordered that they use no lights and that they try to sleep for the remainder of the night, then he sat in an armchair that he had moved over to the bay window and he dozed as the others found comfortable bedrooms and slept deeply until the sun rose the following morning.

Lizzie had woken first and using the portable stove she prepared a 'fry-up' of eggs, tinned tomatoes, and baked beans.

The aroma of the cooking stirred Garner who, although he had been aware of Lizzie's movements in the kitchen, had remained deep in the armchair, feeling quite relaxed.

After a satisfying and filling breakfast he told the two youngsters that they could spend the day on the pebbly beach, providing that they did not stray any further than some fifty yards from the B&B, and he gave them a pressurised air klaxon that he had found in the hallway cupboard.

"Here. Any trouble. Any danger. You use this" he told them, "It'll make enough noise to get me running".

It was a beautiful sunny morning so Sammy and Tom, holding hands, went down on to the beach and they lay, on a blanket that they had brought with them, in the lee of a wooden dinghy that was drawn up from the edge of the lapping waves of a gentle sea.

They communicated in awkward ways and seemed to understand each other, and they lay and dozed peacefully in the warmth of the morning sun.

Garner and Lizzie checked over their supplies and then, his Browning held loosely in his hand, he led the nurse on a tour of the houses and bungalows, searching for signs of recent life, messages, information, and above all, more non-perishable foods, as he had no idea when they might get to a supermarket again.

Dougal went too, led by Lizzie, holding the small dog on a lead made of string.

After a couple of hours lazing and enjoying the sun, and finding out more about Sammy, Tom was suddenly startled by the sound of a sharp crack that caused him to automatically dip his head.

"What was that?" Tom exclaimed, looking puzzled at Sammy, who was looking around to see for herself.

Sammy was further surprised and startled when he grabbed her and dragged her low into the shaded underside of the dinghy.

"Whhh . . . ." Sammy gurgled pitifully.

Tom had sensed danger.

He held her down, his body shielding hers.

"Don't move. I think somebody's throwing stones at us" he said.

Tom had heard a thud in the wooden side of the boat immediately after hearing the sharp crack, and he had assumed that it was a pebble.

It had been very close to his head.

"Where's the klaxon?" Tom now asked Sammy.

"Here" Sammy put it in his hand and she flinched, covering her ears with both hands, as he squeezed the trigger to release an awful screeching sound that echoed across the small bay.

Garner, just leaving a tidy bungalow with the nurse, heard the signal and he raced towards the beach, running low and using every obstacle as a shield, sensing danger himself.

Lizzie started to follow but stopped dead after Garner rasped out an order for her to stay where she was, and to "Stay low".

Cautiously he made his way across the beach, his feet sliding noisily in the pebbles, making his way to where he could see Sammy and Tom laying very still beside a dinghy.

Sweat ran down his temples as a fear of the youngster being gravely injured entered his thoughts.

His eyes were darting at every possible source of threat, but he saw nothing.

Getting nearer to his daughter he swallowed hard, holding back a cry, thinking her dead for she had not moved.

Thinking the worst Garner cried out, "Sammy" and he fell to his knees beside her.

Sammy suddenly sat up and clung tightly to her father as Tom began to tell him of his fears that someone was "throwing stones at them".

Tom felt along the side of the boat as Garner continued to search for any attackers.

"Something hit the boat. Here, I think. I heard a sharp crack first then a thudding sound" Tom told him.

Garner felt that there was no one near who might have attacked the couple and his eyes wandered to the dinghy and he studied the area where Tom had been feeling.

He discovered a fresh splintered scarring and a bullet hole.

"Down!" Garner rasped and he fell across them both, his Browning held in readiness.

He looked around again.

From under Garner's muscled body Tom was heard to venture, "What's up?"

Garner remained silent and he continued to study all around, particularly the direction that a shot could have originated.

He did not want to frighten the youngsters by telling them the facts.

"Stay down. Keep very low. Do not move until I tell you" he said and they heard him move away, his steps making crunching noises on the pebbles.

Moving from the beached vessels he made his way up the beach towards the steep side of the bay.

Suspecting that the mysterious gunman had used the cliffs as his position, Garner moved up the cliff path, upwards and slowly, his movements now ultra cautious and using his experience and training.

There were many positions on the shrubby slopes of the cliff path that a gunman could have used and Garner studied every one before moving on.

Then, at a sharp turn in the path he found where the gunman had watched and then had fired at the youngsters.

He was not really surprised to find the stubs of cheroots as well as the spent bullet case.

Kneeling close to the ground he picked the brass case up and put it in his pocket, then continuing his search he moved stealthily up the cliff path until he came to the top and found the terrain extremely open all around.

From this point Garner found that he could see for miles and as he looked landwards he spotted a movement far off where a line of trees ran parallel to a road.

Squinting in the bright sunlight Garner saw what appeared to be a sports car running silently downhill until it disappeared.

He then heard the distant sound of the car's engine starting and then becoming fainter as the car drove further inland.

"Who are you, you bastard?" Garner muttered.

Deciding that it was the mysterious gunman, garner backtracked and ushered Sammy and Tom back to the B&B where Lizzie met them.

Time for the truth now, he decided, and he told all three of them what he suspected.

He was still puzzled in some respects.

Why?

What was the reason for the stalking?

He suspected that the gunman, using the type of weapon that he also suspected was being used, could easily have hit Tom.

Or Sammy.

But why did'nt he?

What was he, or she, up to?

Sammy and Tom sat together in the cosy drawing room, each of them perplexed and a little frightened by what Garner had told them.

They all showered after Garner found that the B&B had it's own oil fired boiler.

So after getting the system to function properly, hot water was to be in abundance.

During that evening the youngsters talked quietly as the dog Dougal sat on Sammy's lap enjoying the fussing that both youngsters were giving him.

The little dog had been with Lizzie, on the string lead, during all of the 'excitement' earlier.

The nurse, then Garner, showered, then after a quick easy meal which he thoroughly enjoyed, the two adults stood out on the veranda and looked out to sea, talking in quiet tones.

Leaning side by side on the rail they discovered for the first time some things about each other that before there had been no time for.

Lizzie now felt that she knew him better and she felt more trust and confidence in his aims to get them all to a place of safety.

Garner discovered now that Lizzie had been a nurse since leaving college and had never married.

"I was in a relationship" she told him as she studied the horizon, "but it did'nt last very long. He cheated on me with my best friend. I suppose the experience put me off the opposite sex for a while, and then this awful epidemic suddenly took over my life".

Before that she had cared for her disabled widowed father, a retired schoolteacher, who was suffering from Parkinson's disease.

Lizzie had been juggling her caring for her father during her relationship, and then he had been one of the first to die when the virus ran riot in the UK.

"So, I had no one" she continued, "And when I was asked to help out at the prison I gladly went along".

Garner studied her features in the glow of the evening sun.

Her freckled face, framed in her full auburn hair, was extremely attractive.

He had not really noticed this before.

How on earth had she managed to keep the men away, especially whilst she had been assisting at the prison hospital?

She was very attractive.

He winced inside, feeling a bit guilty.

She was bloody beautiful!

Garner suddenly realised that he was experiencing feelings that he had not had for some years and felt that it was the wrong time and place to start now.

Startled by his sudden change of mood and a sense of aloofness, Lizzie was surprised when he turned, and saying a grunted "Goodnight" he went into the house, telling her to rest, get a good night's sleep, as they were to continue their journey the next day.

Chapter 16

The night passed quietly enough although the weather was now changing for the worse.

Garner had sat up all night, keeping watch.

Lizzie came quietly to him at 5am and advised him to rest a while, and in fact he fell into a deep sleep until she woke him at 9am.

He allowed them a decent breakfast before organizing them into the packing of essentials into the 4 x 4.

Among the newer items that they packed was a flare gun and flares.

Garner had acquired these when he had sorted a few things out in the small chandlery down by the bay the day before.

What he did realise then was that he had mislaid the shotgun when they had hurried from Squires Manor the night before last.

He studied maps of the locality to define his route to Weymouth, for that would be on the road to his planned destination, should that destination still exist.

After such a pleasant day yesterday, this morning was now heavy with threatening rain clouds and a fierce wind that gusted up the road from the small horseshoe shaped bay.

They were about to leave, sitting ready in the car, when they saw the full beam headlights of a vehicle racing along the road into the little hamlet.

Garner switched the engine off and they sat watching as a small white van approached.

It was being driven very fast and erratically, and before it came parallel with them, parked as they were in front of the B&B, the van veered wildly, hit a low wall, and spun around before crashing, side on, to a halt in the front garden of a neat little bungalow.

Lizzie started to open the door of the 4 x 4 to go to the aid of the driver, a natural reaction, but Garner stopped her and she was forced to sit quietly and watch as smoke rose from the van's crumpled engine.

Garner sat and studied the van, and watched the road behind leading into the village.

After some minutes he decided that the van was alone and he instructed Lizzie and Sammy to leave the car with him, leaving Tom holding Dougal.

Garner had some difficulty in opening the driver's door but eventually he managed it and he and Lizzie pulled the unconscious driver clear, then they carried the man into the bungalow.

The door had previously been forced the day before when Garner and Lizzie were searching the building for valuable and useful equipment, including more foodstuffs.

Lizzie tended the man's injuries and gave him sips of water as he regained consciousness.

The man was a scruffy and unshaven character, but that was to be expected these dark days, and he appeared to be in his mid fifties.

With a voice hoarse and halting the man introduced himself.

"Me name's Joe . . . Joe Bartlett . . . I . . . am . . . sorry, was . . . a farm hand based on a farm outside of Blandford Forum" he told them.

"We were up that way a couple of days ago" Tom said, standing behind Sammy who held his hand again.

Joe nodded, "Yeah . . ." he paused and appeared to be considering what to say.

"I've been running from 'Them' . . . . They must be somewhere behind me . . ." he turned and tried to look out of a low window, a real fear in his bloodshot eyes.

He was obviously terrified of 'Them'!

"We've got to get away quickly. They'll be here . . . soon . . . I . . . I . . . ." and he tailed off his words and closed his eyes.

Then he slowly attempted to get to his feet but his legs gave way.

He cried out with pain.

"Oh, me back . . . me blasted back . . . it's killing me" he cried with a frustration bent with fury.

Lizzie examined him as best she could, trying not to breath in his rancid stale body odour.

She discovered that his lower spine was badly cut and bruised and guessed that something quite serious was going on inside Joe's damaged body.

She shook her head as Garner gave her an enquiring look.

"I don't think you'll be going anywhere for a while yet, Joe" Garner told him.

With Sammy, still holding Tom by the hand, standing at the door and keeping watch on the road, Garner spoke softly to Joe telling that for the present they were safe.

Lizzie continued to dress the many cuts and abrasions that Joe had, including a wide and deep cut under his right shoulder blade.

It reminded her of her own wound, now healing nicely.

Joe, now more relaxed and quieter, explained that he got the injury whilst escaping from "Them" the day before.

As he began to flee, he told them, the apparent leader of "Them", a mad woman in a Nun's habit, had speared him as he raced for the van.

This shook Garner, for it sounded like the same woman who had led the bunch who abducted Sammy and had hit him at the Inn.

How on earth was she travelling about, and with whom?

Garner sat and talked quietly with Joe for the following few minutes, then allowed the exhausted man to sleep.

He had discovered that the "Nun" had led a sizeable group of virus-infected people of both sexes.

Joe might have been exaggerating when he told Garner that he thought that there was about fifty of them.

The poor man had been barely surviving on the farm where he worked, after the farmer and his family had died in the epidemic as it first swept through the UK.

Then, some days ago, the insane mob came.

Joe had hidden as they ransacked the farm, finding very little to satisfy their hunger.

Watching with horror he had witnessed their madness, resorting to cannibalism when finding insufficient food for their group.

This in itself was almost enough to send the poor man mad, but he remained hidden and silently watched their mad antics and their infighting.

He had seen a woman, huge and very stout, arguing bitterly with the Nun who, when her adversary had struck her and then had turned to gloat to the others, had speared her through the back to her front.

Many other insane decadent scenes had been played out before Joe's eyes and finally he could stand no more and he had made his bid for freedom.

Someone must have seen him as he ran silently around the outside of them, through the shrubbery, and that person had begun to wail and shriek like a wild animal.

The others, most of them gathered in the area between the farmhouse and a barn, were now aroused and they began to run after him, baying insanely.

Joe had almost reached his van, hidden round the back of the barn, when he had felt the intense pain in his back, and he had almost fallen.

Joe had paused then as he related all of this to Garner, a dark expression of terror in his eyes.

"She had me . . . . but . . . but . . . suddenly there was a sharp crack . . . like the sound of a gun . . . and a wild man who had just got to me . . . he . . . he fell dead . . . or I think he was . . . for the top of his head had disappeared . . ."

Joe had then managed to get into the van and had locked the doors as the mad throng stood, puzzled and looking around before turning to attack the van as Joe started it up and drove through them and out and away from the farm.

He knew that he had injured some, many of them seriously, as he flew in horror from the farm but he was now driving madly himself at a terrific speed down the country lanes to get as far from there as possible.

At first Joe had seen them chasing him in three vehicles, the headlights blazing, but gradually he had got further in front until, and he confessed that he had relaxed perhaps too early, and that morning he had seen them in the distance closing on him.

"I think I lost them again back at the junction . . . but I'm not absolutely sure . . . ." Joe had continued.

Garner studied the outskirts of the village and the road leading down to it.

Where were they now?

A bit of advanced planning was now required.

Chapter 17

Garner checked his watch.

It was just after eleven.

Leaving them all in the bungalow he crept out of the back door and scouted away from the road towards the main arterial route leading down to Lulworth.

The browning automatic was tucked in the waistband of his trousers and as an additional weapon he held the flare gun in one hand.

The weather had worsened and gusty winds blew squally rain inland from the sea.

He halted as the buildings petered out and the road became a lane with hedges either side, and fields and trees beyond them.

Ahead on a gradual bend in the road stood a garage with six fuel pumps under a high roof.

Using the cover of the hedge, running along the edge of a field, Garner made his way to the garage.

No sign of life there, and he found that looters had got into the shop area at some time, wrecking it and leaving drinks and confectionary spread across the shop floor.

A plan was building in his mind.

At the back of the wide concrete platform that the garage was built upon stood a delivery tanker.

Garner checked the on-board volume meter and determined that there was still some petrol inside the tank.

Luckily the keys were still in the ignition, so he climbed up onto the cab and started the tanker's engine, then he drove it out of the garage so that it blocked the road leading into the little hamlet.

Making sure that the only access now, down the road, to the bay was through the garage, Garner opened the valve of the tanker and petrol gushed from the tank, soon flooding the road.

Holding his handkerchief over his mouth to keep the strong acrid fumes of the petrol out, he ran into the garage and managed to get two of the pumps to run their contents free, washing across the concrete apron and to the roadway.

High grade petrol and diesel flooded together.

Now with the garage forecourt awash with fuel he began to backtrack down the lane towards the nearest buildings.

It was just in time.

He was suddenly aware of the sound of vehicles approaching.

The bright beams of headlights swept the hedges as three vehicles, the first was an open backed truck, followed by two vans of the people carrier type.

Garner saw clearly that the occupants in the back of the open-back truck were obviously of the insane type, their clothes and particularly their ravaged faces giving it away.

They rushed speedily towards the bend in the road upon which the garage stood.

Garner stayed hidden beside the first bungalow further down the lane.

The three vehicles came around the bend then slowed as the driver saw the tanker blocking the way.

After initial hesitation the truck was revved up and came on, turning into the garage.

The other two vehicles followed.

As the leading vehicle got to the garage exit, having navigated the pumps and other obstacles, Garner stood up and taking careful aim he fired the flare gun directly at the roadway where the tanker had disgorged it's lethal contents.

There was a terrific explosion and the leading vehicle roared out of the flames with it's tyres aflame.

Then the garage exploded with an enormous blast and the two following vans were totally engulfed.

A man had leapt from the rear of the third van and was running in the direction where Garner stood.

The ragged newcomer held a wicked looking machete and he stopped just yards from Garner and raised the weapon, about to attack.

Garner had been deafened by the blast and had kept his eyes on the first vehicle as it passed him to race madly down towards the bay.

And he was completely unaware of the impending attack.

Then, amid the deafening roaring of the fire a sharp crack sounded out and the mad man fell dead.

Garner had not noticed this at all.

The vans and their occupants were completely obliterated by the explosion and terrible screams were loud, but very short as the victims died.

Still with the flare gun in his hand Garner raced urgently back to the bungalow where he had left the others.

The open-back truck had passed this bungalow where Sammy and the others remained out of sight.

Garner crashed through the door.

"Quick. Get in the car. NOW! Hurry!" he ordered them.

Each grabbed their loose packs, Tom hugging the dog tightly, and they rushed out to board the 4 x 4.

Joe was far too ill to move, so Garner gave the man his Browning and promised to do his best and return or send help, as soon as he could.

"Look. I can't take you now" he said, "Use the gun if you have to. Don't hesitate. I'm sorry to leave you but . . . well, you know I can't take you with us . . . ." His voice tailed off.

He felt really bad about it.

Seeing this Joe realised his predicament but bravely accepted it.

"Go on. You go. I'll be alright" he studied the weapon that Garner had given him, "I'll get a few with this . . . ."

Feeling almost sick about leaving Joe, for Garner was not one to desert anybody, he wished the man the best of luck and ran outside and joined the others.

Starting the 4 x 4 he turned it quickly in the road and slammed his foot to the floor, causing the heavy tyres to grip the gravelled road and squeal as he sped off.

He had noted earlier a narrow unmade track, about a hundred yards up the road, and from his scanning of a local map he knew that the track led to rough hilly country that followed the coastline.

And it led in the right direction that he felt he had to go to enable him to pass on the vital paperwork and vaccine to a proper authority at a destination suggested by old Robert Cecil before he died.

An old wooden gate barred the way onto the track so he steered directly at it and easily crashed through to go haring along the grassy rutted lane.

Reaching a rise, where the track wound around a bend leading towards the sea, Garner stopped and they all looked back over the small hamlet they had just fled from.

Back at the bungalow one of the surviving mob had discovered Joe, laying alone on the carpet, his shoulders up against the wall.

The filthy man called the others in a strange guttural voice.

With sweat dripping from his brow, some of it caused by his fever and some by fear, Joe waited for them to attack.

Terrified, but with a little confidence whilst holding the gun, he saw them rush into the room where he lay, and holding the Browning with both hands Joe aimed and pulled the trigger.

The weapon roared and he fired again.

Two of them fell as they rushed him, screaming insanely, but he was suddenly speared through the stomach by the black garbed figure of a Nun.

As Joe lay dying, the long weapon protruding from his stomach, he saw through misting eyes the Nun take a Samurai sword from it's bracket on the wall.

He just did not care as he saw her approach him and sweep the weapon in the air.

The last thing that Joe heard was her shrill cackle of triumph as she sliced his head from his body.

Garner and his small band of fugitives had been looking as the trucks and the garage burnt furiously, a great plume of black smoke crawled slowly upwards and hung hundreds of feet in the rain sodden air.

Garner had seen the lead vehicle stop at the edge of the beach and it's three occupants were out of it and moving up the road.

The vehicle was now well alight and it's fuel exploded adding to the general roar of flames and hot spinning metal.

He took the binoculars found in the chandlery and focused on the three mad people as they entered the bungalow.

"Bloody Hell!" he said loud enough for the others to hear.

"What?" Lizzie asked, a frown on her face.

"It's the bloody Nun!" Garner exclaimed, "Where the bloody hell did she come from?"

Faintly they heard two sharp shots coming from the bungalow, and then an insane shriek.

It went deathly quiet down at the bungalow.

Then, "Oh, No!" Garner murmured.

For just then he saw as the Nun came out of the bungalow alone, waving a huge shining sword in her left hand, and a head in the other.

Quickly Garner focused on her right hand and tears came to his eyes.

The head was Joes!

Garner watched as the Nun wailed and screamed incoherently at the sea, swinging the head around as if it was a trophy.

But she was alone.

At least poor old Joe had taken a few with him.

"C'mon. Let's keep going" Garner said and they were rammed back in their seats as he floored the accelerator and drove fast further up the rise towards the cliff edge paths.

Watching through binoculars from a hill across the valley the man with the sophisticated rifle slung across his shoulders smiled as he saw the 4 x 4 disappear along the track near a cliff edge.

Turning to watch the Nun for a moment the man then went over to a racy sports car, started it up, and after lighting a thin cheroot and taking in a few deep drag of the acrid tasting tobacco, he steered the car out onto a road and drove slowly westwards.

Chapter 18

The weather improved slightly as Garner drove them across the cliff tops, but the wind was still fierce.

The rough grassy track ran close to the cliff edge and Lizzie became quite nervous as she was sitting beside Garner in the front of the 4 x 4.

From her position Lizzie was looking down to the sea where the waves crashed over submerged rocks, so she closed her eyes.

The coastal track ran uphill and then down, following the contours of the coastline.

They reached the top of a steep uphill drive and Garner pulled up to survey the coast and land ahead.

Lizzie had opened her eyes and was looking around generally.

"Look. Look, Ron . . . ." she exclaimed and pointed to their right.

Garner and Sammy turned to find what Lizzie had seen.

Bounding up from a grassy slope came a thin looking lioness, followed by two very young lion cubs, one of them limping badly and struggling to keep up.

The lioness stopped a few yards away from the vehicle and began to walk up and down as if rating the chances of food being offered.

The healthiest cub sat watching it's mother as the other, lame, cub caught up and lay down beside it's sibling.

The occupants of the 4 x 4 watched this for a few minutes then Garner spoke quietly.

"We have'nt anything that we could give them, so we had better move on".

"Oh" Lizzie said, "Is'nt it a shame?"

"Pass me the klaxon, Sam" Garner turned to his daughter.

Sammy reached into her rucksack and found the klaxon, then handed it to Garner.

He wound his window down and the lioness's ears pricked up and she took a step towards the vehicle.

Garner said, "Bye!" and released air from the klaxon's canister and the resulting high shriek sent all three animals running away back down the hill.

"How did they get here, d'you think?" Lizzie ask Garner.

"I should imagine that as their keeper's became too ill to care for them and perhaps could do no more for them, they released them to the wild" Garner mused.

Then using his binoculars he swept the area from left to right and saw nothing that might tempt him to go in any other direction.

Sammy had watched as the lioness and her cubs ran down the hill and into a copse of tall poplars.

She then looked back again at the sea.

She suddenly yelped in her strange way and pointed downwards to the sea a little ahead of them.

The other turned their attention to where she was pointing and they saw a concrete causeway running into the sea from a landward location out of their sight at present, but further along the track on which they were driving.

Alongside the causeway was a small luxury cruiser, moored and rolling in the waves that washed up the causeway.

Garner could see that the track ahead dropped sharply and appeared to approach an inlet where the causeway must originate landside.

He drove slowly downwards, it was extremely steep here, but he felt confident in the 4 x 4, and he followed the track as it turned first inland, following the line of a fence, then through an open gate, and out onto a very narrow, tarmac-surfaced, lane.

Turning left he drove slowly down towards the sea.

On the right hand side of the road, around a bend with steep grassed slopes either side, appeared two small buildings.

One was a well-kept cottage and the other was a boathouse, recently built and a little larger.

Garner drew up outside of the cottage, turned the engine off and, ordering the others to remain in the vehicle, he got out cautiously and approached the front door of the cottage.

The door was closed and he could not open it so he went around the building, peering in the windows as he went.

Garner tapped on the windows, just in case there was somebody inside but by the time he had got round to the back he was convinced that the place was empty.

Reaching the rear where there was a small kitchen garden he tried the back door and found that it was unlocked and he opened it and went inside.

Searching all of the rooms he found no signs of life or recent habitation, so he unbolted the front door and signalled for the others to come in.

There was a small sitting-room, nicely furnished, and the fireplace was prepared with a few logs, so he started a fire there before going into the kitchen where he lit a fire in the grate of an old cast iron range.

Within a couple of hours the cottage was warm and snug and the girls fell asleep, Sammy in a fireside armchair, and Lizzie stretched out on the settee facing the fire in the sitting-room.

Tom, with Dougal on his lap, sat dozing in another armchair by the fire.

Not ready to rest yet Garner left the cottage and went into the boathouse.

It was filled with much boating paraphernalia, including a robust looking inflatable that had a powerful outboard engine fitted at the stern.

Checking the fuel tank Garner discovered that it was full.

Once again an idea was forming in his head.

Going out to the causeway he leapt into the cruiser, which was securely moored, and he found that it too had plenty of fuel in its tank.

Checking the interior he considered that the owner of this craft must have been quite well off, for it was the luxurious type of cruiser you would find in an expensive marina.

The owner probably owned the cottage and boathouse as well.

The cruiser was quite big, about eighteen feet in length and fitted out very comfortably.

Garner now dashed back to the cottage, as the rain was falling heavily now, rushing in torrents down the lane and into the sea.

Once inside the cottage he dried himself and then sat at the kitchen table and studied a map of the coast, making notes on a pad, and a list of essentials that he considered they must take, heading the list "PORTLAND".

He then lay his head on his arms and fell into a deep sleep.

It was dark outside and still raining heavily when he awoke, smelling the beefy aroma of a pot of stew, made from tins of soup and a few potatoes that the nurse had boiled and was now heating on the stove.

Looking at his wristwatch he saw that it was not yet six o'clock in the evening.

He and Lizzie sat in silence and ate some of the stew, and then they sat quietly talking until eight when he decided that it was time to wake Sammy and Tom.

He allowed the youngsters to eat a little of the stew before telling them all about his plan to leave the 4 x 4 and sail in the cruiser to the Royal Navy's base at Portland Bill where he felt sure that there must be some military organisation who could advise him what to do and where to make for with the priority info that he was carrying, and also a safe destination for the girls and Tom.

"Do we really have to go by sea?" Lizzie groaned, "Only I'm not a very good sailor and I get seasick easily" she told him.

With a wicked grin on his face Garner told her, "Tough! You'll just have to bear it, Lizzie".

And he continued by telling her that it was probably the safest way, and more direct to his destination ultimately.

"I'm sorry but that's it. I'll get you all there as soon as I can" he continued, "Get some rest now and we'll leave at first light in the morning".

So, with the weather still atrocious, they bedded down for the night and slept fitfully during a stormy night.

Garner allowed them to sleep late again as it was still blowing hard rain in from the sea and huge boiling waves were crashing way up the causeway and almost up to the boathouse.

Finally it was late morning when he woke them and waited while they ate a breakfast of cereals with long-life milk, although Lizzie refrained, feeling a little nauseous already.

The bad weather had abated and now there was a slight wind, broken clouds, and a little sunshine.

Using the list he had written the previous day they took the bare essentials from the 4x4, and the cottage, and transferred it all to the moored cruiser.

Garner went back into the cottage where he checked all around; collected a few remaining items, and then went out to the boathouse where he had told the others to wait.

Garner organised them and they helped him to wheel the inflatable out and down the causeway where he attached it to the stern of the cruiser.

Then, taking his time as Sammy, Lizzie, Tom, and Dougal got aboard the cruiser; he climbed a nearby cliff-path to a high point where he could study the immediate terrain.

Seeing nothing untoward Garner slid back down to the cruiser, climbed aboard and started the engine.

There was some coughing and clunking from the engine accompanied by a few clouds of black smoke, and then it seemed to settle down to a steady chugging.

Garner cast off and was soon steering seawards, away from the inlet.

Looking at his watch he noted that it was now nearly two in the afternoon.

It had taken longer than he expected to transfer all that they needed to the boats.

The cruiser was nearing the headland where he would steer around and follow the coast, when a sports car came quietly, as if in neutral, around the bend in the lanr and stopped some way up from the 4 x 4.

The driver, his rifle still slung across his back, crept furtively towards the cottage, and then moved over to check the 4 x 4.

He peered inside and then, as the wind lessened, he heard the faint sound of the cruiser's engine out at sea.

Quickly bringing a pair of binoculars to bear on the boat, the man saw Garner at the wheel and the others sitting in the saloon area.

With a terrible gust of hatred the man cursed and kicked hard at the tyres of the 4 x 4 as he realised that for now his quarry was getting further away from him.

He crashed through the front door of the cottage and searched wildly for some clue as to where Garner and Co. were heading.

Then, he found it . . . . the pad that Garner had written on, and there at the top of a blank page, the pencil's indention quite plain to see.

"PORTLAND, Eh?" That's where they were going.

The man smiled and casually lit a cheroot before sauntering back to his car.

He stood watching as the cruiser disappeared around the headland, then he ground the cheroot under his boot, got in the car and drove slowly back up the lane.

The cruiser sailed steadily along the coast and Garner was beginning to relax, thinking that they were nearing the end of their adventure, when suddenly and without warning there was a horrible loud grinding sound from the engine and a cloud of black smoke rose from the engine hatch.

The cruiser slowed and began to roll in the swell.

Running to the hatch Garner opened it and the others heard him swearing and grunting before coming up to inform them that "The bloody things knackered. It must have been tied up for some maintenance" he belatedly observed.

Already Lizzie was being violently sick, vomiting copiously over the side.

Garner climbed into the inflatable and checked the engine.

He started it, and it ran smoothly.

"Right. Come on. Get in . . . . quickly now" he ordered the others.

And he got them to pass their essential supplies to him as they joined him in the inflatable.

The cruiser was then abandoned and he steered away, continuing the route along the coast.

Lizzie continued to be sick, hanging dangerously over the side with both Tom and Sammy holding on to her.

The sea spray soaked her upper body and was particularly cold.

Dougal lay shivering beneath the seat that Tom sat on.

It had begun to rain again and within minutes they were all soaking wet before they had the chance to don the proper wet proof clothing that they had brought along.

Drenched and cold they sat silently as the inflatable sped along, rolling in the ever increasing swell.

It seemed a long journey, what with the events earlier and the transfer from one craft to another, and it began to grow dark.

Garner studied the shoreline and in the fading light, through persistent rain, he recognised the town of Weymouth to his right.

It seemed odd to see the once vibrant seaside town in complete darkness.

Not one light showed anywhere.

Approaching Portland Bill, Garner steered the inflatable towards the entrance to the Naval Dockyard.

By the time that he had entered the Dockyard it had become totally dark, but they were very glad to be in calm waters within the huge harbour.

But, encouragingly, there were lights showing in the main admin. building.

He slowed and steered to a set of stone steps that led up to the quayside above them.

Stopping the engine he made the craft secure and was about to step out of the craft when a sudden shot startled them all and they ducked for cover.

A voice called out "Stay exactly where you are. DO NOT MOVE!!"

Chapter 19

Sammy and Lizzie shrank down to the bottom of the inflatable, hugging each other in fear.

Tom held Dougal tightly, looking about with sightless eyes, fearful but curious.

Garner was somewhat annoyed, to say the least.

They were all soaking wet and cold and the fact that someone, obviously armed, was now obstructing their way to shelter and warmth steeled him to a real anger.

For a moment he contemplated rushing up the slippery stone steps, but he sensibly held himself in check and waited for the next move.

The sound of steel clad boots could now be heard, and getting closer, and in the darkness and drizzle Garner made out the shape of a small group of figures marching along the quay towards the head of the steps.

Out of this gloom and drizzle and into the light that illuminated the area above them came four uniformed men led by a tall gangly figure.

The men had shouldered their weapons and their officer, as he turned out to be, held a service pistol in his hand.

"Who are you? Where are you from? And more importantly do you have anyone with you who is, or seems to be ill?" the pistol bearing officer rapped out those three questions in a demanding tone.

"We are four and seeking some safety and support. We've come from London via the southern counties." Garner called up to the man, "We've also had to avoid a few groups of very strange and dangerous types, and 'No' we do not have anyone here who is ill or even suspected of being ill. Does that answer your question?"

"Right then" the officer said in a loud authoritative manner, his Scottish accent very strong, "You'd better come up then. And take care. Those steps are slippery".

As they stood up to leave the inflatable they heard the officer add, "You maybe OK but we must be sure, so when you all reach the quayside, stay close together and follow me at ten paces behind. My men with then follow you . . . . at a distance".

Garner assisted the others from the inflatable and up the steps where they stood in a group.

"You appear to be OK, probably like us 'normals' but we will need to get you checked over" The Scot continued.

Garner had not heard this term before.

The Officer led off and Garner followed him with the girls, Tom and Dougal staying close. Sammy, as usual, had taken Tom by the hand and kept him with her as they all followed the officer, with his four armed men a way behind them.

They were then escorted around the L-shaped quayside to the main Administration Building.

As the steel door clanged shut behind them they became aware of the warmth and the mouth-watering aroma of something cooking.

The Naval party's leader, the Chief Petty Officer with the strong Glasgow accent, introduced himself to them as they continued to follow him.

"My name's Patterson" he told them, directing his words to Garner, "CPO Patterson".

They had reached the bottom of a flight of steel stairs that led up to a platform.

CPO Patterson stopped and signalled for one of the escort party to step forward.

"Would you ladies and the young man with the doggie please go with Randall, here.

He will take you to our isolation room first where you will be examined by our Doctor Meltis." He paused and turning to Garner he said, "And you, sir, will you follow me.

Commander Richards would like a word"

Tom and the girls went off with the young naval rating, Sammy watching her father as he began to follow CPO Patterson up the stairway.

Garner and the CPO reached the higher platform where there was a secure looking door with a window in it.

CPO Patterson entered a code in the key-pad set beside the door and he then led Garner into a vast control room.

The room had wide windows that gave panoramic views of the bay to seaward on one side, and the inner dockyard and landwards on the other.

There were seven persons, all naval personnel, positioned at computers and high tech. Communications equipment.

One of these persons, a stocky grey haired officer, rose to meet them.

The man looked exhausted, but apart from that he was immaculately dressed in the uniform of a Lieutenant Commander of the Royal Navy.

"Hello." He said in a tired but friendly tone, "I'm Stuart Richards, newly made leader of our small heroic band. And you are?" he held out his hand.

Garner took his hand and shook it.

"Garner, sir. Was until recently sergeant in the Rifles, sir" he lied.

Richards smiled wryly.

"Give me a brief history of your recent activities. How far have you come, and why here?" Commander Richards asked him.

Leaving out his incarceration in prison Garner told him of their travels since leaving London, including their near contact with the infected types, and of his desire to get his daughter, Lizzie, and Tom to a place of safety.

"Right. Well, let's get you checked out physically, fed and watered, and then we will see what next" the Commander said. "I'll take you down to see our resident doctor, Doctor Meltis. He's a good chap. One of the old school."

"Stay up here, will you, Patterson, old chap. I'll go with Mr. Garner to the doctor" and he led Garner out of the control room and down the stairs.

On the way the Commander told Garner how all of his superiors had perished with the 'bloody virus' leaving him in charge.

"I don't know how or why the rest of us have survived it, but we have" he continued, then, "Ah, here we are . . . ."

During the chatting they had walked along a low-lit corridor, not far, and were now outside a door with the sign, "Medics".

They entered the large ward-like room, with four beds on either side and an examination room at the end.

The girls and Tom, still holding Dougal, sat on one of the beds near the examination room.

A very short bald man wearing a long white coat that was too long for him, and the sleeves rolled up, peered over half-lens spectacles at the new visitor.

The commander guided Garner over to meet the doctor.

"You must be the youngster's father?" the doctor stammered.

Garner nodded and said "Yes, is she . . . are they alright?" he asked.

"Oh, Yes. They're fine. It's so nice to find some healthy civilians for a change" doctor Meltis replied, stammering again.

"Right. Doctor Meltis, would you check Mr.Garner, here, see if he is OK too?"

The Commander said, "He looks and acts fine to me. I'm sure he's OK".

Garner was told to follow the doctor into the examination area and the Commander followed.

As Garner was examined he noticed how the Commander helped himself to a couple of glasses of Scotch, poured from a bottle he had taken from a wall cupboard.

Garner noticed how the Commander's hands shook as he poured the amber liquid.

He had noticed during their brief walk together how the Commander's breath smelled of alcohol.

The Commander sat on a vacant bunk and continued to talk as Garner was thoroughly examined by Doctor Meltis.

"Yes. You may have noticed that I do not have very many personnel upstairs in the control room".

Garner remembered seeing three wrens and three male ratings in the control room with the Commander when he had walked in.

Sitting back with his glass held high the Commander continued.

"I'm afraid that we are not in a very strong position at present" he said, "There are twenty-one personnel on site, some of them at present posted around the area on patrol and on sentry duty. We are constantly plagued by attempts being made by the "Crazies" to invade and take over the large food and weapons stores here".

He paused to empty the Scotch down his throat in one gulp.

"Only yesterday . . . . it was yesterday, was'nt it, Meltis? . . . . only yesterday, we were attacked by a mob of about seventy mixed "Crazies", and I lost a young rating killed, another seriously injured, and two slightly hurt. But they had killed over twenty of the attackers before they ran back in the direction of Weymouth."

Enquiring about the chances of any reinforcements Garner was told that they were in contact with one of the few military controlled areas in England and a force of armed personnel were due within the week to relieve them.

Recognising that getting the information regarding the vaccine to the proper authority as being of the most importance, Commander Richards discussed the possibilities with Garner, explaining that he knew that there was a scientist at the main military base, working on possible answers to the virus.

This base that he referred to was in the middle of the Dorset countryside, the Commander told Garner.

It was just as Garner had believed all along.

"How do I get there?" he asked the Commander as Doctor Meltis finished examining him and he put his damp shirt back on.

"Well. We have a fully equipped Lynx helicopter in hangar three . . . . , but unfortunately nobody who can fly it".

Commander Richards handed the empty glass to the doctor, "Thank you, Doc" he said, then continuing, "It would be the best way to get to the base as it is too bloody dangerous overland, as you well know now" he said to Garner.

Garner smiled.

"I was trained as a helicopter pilot, sir" he lied, "And it was the Lynx that we used from time to time".

"Ah! That is fortunate" Commander Richards rubbed his hands together, "Let's get your ladies and the lad fed and made comfortable first. We'll get them some replacements clothing, then you and I, and CPO Patterson, will have a chat. Make some arrangement for you to go . . . with our Lynx."

He escorted them to a small canteen and they were fed with warm nourishing food served at a table by a smart young wren.

Afterwards CPO took them to the showers where they luxuriated in the warm jets of water and pleasant soaps.

Then dressed in various clean and new naval clothing the girls and Tom were led to a dormitory where they were allowed to rest before falling asleep.

Garner was once again invited to sit with the Commander and CPO Patterson in an office, where they arranged the plans for Garner and his team to fly off the next day.

They were also to take the seriously injured sailor with them.

Sitting comfortably at the office table, and sharing a bottle of Scotch Malt Whisky, Garner began to let the feeling of exhaustion take him over and after they had agreed a plan, he said goodnight and was escorted to the dormitory where he fell instantly asleep on a bunk next to his Sammy.

Although they all slept on short bunk style beds, the mattresses were comfortable and they felt snug and warm, drifting into a deep sleep for the first time in days, knowing that they were quite secure in the safety of the armed base.

They were all wakened the following morning, at seven-thirty, by a young sailor who took them to the canteen where they ate heartily, a breakfast of eggs and bacon together with other fried specialities.

The Commander, together with CPO Patterson in tow, came to speak with Garner, taking him to a separate table, leaving the others sipping their tea or coffee.

It had been an uneventful night, said the Commander, but his guards had spotted a gathering of the "Crazies" up on the grassy slopes that ran down to the bay from the old fort.

Garner was handed a large leather wallet that contained papers that Commander Richards wanted delivered to the Navy's senior officer at the Dorset base.

"Well, Garner" Commander Richards stood and he held out his hand as Garner got to his feet, "Good luck, old chap. I'll leave you with CPO Patterson now. He'll take you and your people to the Lynx, Goodbye". And he turned and left the canteen.

Now filled with good cooked food all four of them, and Dougal, followed the CPO to their temporary quarters where they collected their various items of property, then they followed him out and along a number of underground tunnels where miles of different sized piping ran in all directions.

An echo sounded as their footsteps clanged loudly along steel walkways and stairs.

The hum of generators could be heard in the distance.

Keeping pace behind the CPO they followed him along one of these tunnels before finally ascending more steel stairs and finding themselves now in a huge hangar, aptly called "Number Three Shed" by the CPO.

Huge racks lined the walls containing bits of naval equipment.

And there were areas where work benches stood and various tooling were lined in neat lines on shelves.

Enormous sliding doors were closed in one wall, and immediately before them stood the Lynx helicopter.

A maintenance crew of two ratings were active around the aircraft checking it over before it was to be used by Garner and his party.

He had been advised of the route that he should fly during his discussions with the Commander earlier and now he was handed a clip-board that contained an aerial map for his use.

He studied it as the CPO ordered the maintenance crew to assist the 'laddie' and his 'doggie', and the ladies, on board the helicopter.

Then the seriously injured sailor, strapped to a stretcher was put aboard and belted to the floor, his comrades wishing him "Good Luck" and "Best of Luck".

Garner then shook hands with the CPO who gave him a webbed belt containing a service revolver in a holster, and spare ammunition.

Wishing Garner luck the CPO saluted and turned smartly away to order the men to open the hangar doors.

The helicopter was then wheeled out to the take-off circle, surrounded by a party of armed sailors, swinging their automatic weapons from side to side and looking out for any signs of trouble.

Checking that everyone was securely strapped in their seats, Garner signalled for the ground crews to close the door of the aircraft, then Lizzie locked it as she had been shown earlier.

Donning the helmet and the communications equipment Garner then went about the instrument checking procedure that he remembered from his illegal training in the old days whilst in Afghanistan.

Feeling fairly familiar with the controls and instruments Garner took a deep breath and started the engines.

His memory had served him well and the engines roared into life without him having any embarrassing moments.

Slowly, after minutes of allowing the powerful engines to smoothly reach take-off pitch, he lifted the craft up and for a short moments it swayed a little from side to side, before he managed to coax it to an altitude he was happy with then he turned and flew across the inner harbour towards land.

Commander Richards had been watching from the control room and was secretly relieved to see the helicopter rise successfully and then glide easily away.

He had suspected that Garner had been 'spinning him a yarn', for to his knowledge it was not usual to train soldiers to fly helicopter in the Rifle Brigade, unless of course they were part of a secret group, like the SAS.

But the man seemed genuine enough and certainly would not chance his flying skills if his daughter was with him, so it must be true.

Flying low enough over a mob on the slopes he saw the upturned crazed features of the mixed crowd.

Garner estimated their number and reported it back to the naval base where the mob was obviously heading.

Then he lifted the helicopter up and over the top of the slope and they were now over Weymouth harbour.

They all looked down at the deserted quayside and the large sea-going ferries, and then they were over the town that once bustled with the thousands of visitors usually there at this time of year.

Even through the engine noise they sensed the eeriness of the deserted town.

Garner flew the aircraft inland, then he turned West for a while, fairly low and looking for signs of any normality.

Garner saw it first.

A sports car speeding along the coast road that led to Abbottsbury.

He turned the helicopter and followed it, feeling more at ease with the craft now and confident of his ability.

Flying past and over the car Garner swung it around to face the vehicle, trying to get the driver to respond.

The car stopped and Garner hovered over it expecting the occupant to reveal himself, but nobody got out, so after a minute or two Garner turned inland and sped off, puzzled by the fact that the driver had not shown himself.

Then he remembered.

The "Crazies" could drive.

They had experienced this a few days earlier.

Must have been a "Crazie" then, he thought and concentrated on his flight path strapped to his knee.

He studied the terrain looking for landmarks high-lighted for him on the map.

As the helicopter sped away the car driver got out of the car and watched it through binoculars until it was out of sight.

Smiling, the man lit up the usual cheroot and leaned on the hood of the car, smoking.

Then before driving off, the man studied a road map and worked out where he would make for next.

In his mind he believed he knew where the helicopter was making for.

Meanwhile as they flew over the rolling fields and hills of Southern England they were met with sights that they had not seen during their journey by car and boat.

Here and there, in the corner of fields, lay groups of dead animals.

Dead through neglect caused by the death of their keepers.

Sammy pointed excitedly as she spotted a pride of lions, led by a huge maned male, roaming the farm lands.

The lioness and her cubs that they had encountered on the cliffs outside Lulworth could have come from this pride.

Lizzie explained that the animals were probably from private zoos and had been released from captivity by their dying keepers.

It was mid-morning when Garner recognised the military base that was their destination and after a bumpy landing in the fenced off compound, they were met by an armed group of individuals clothed in heavy space-like overalls and helmets.

Not a word was spoken as Garner's party was escorted into a windowless concrete building, then into a huge lift that took them deep into the heart of the complex.

The doors finally opened and they were ushered out to be met by five uniformed individuals.

These people represented all the three main military services and Garner did not recognise any of them until an army colonel, whose back was turned as he spoke to another officer, turned and smiled and said, "Why. Hello Sergeant Garner. And how are you, old chap?"

Coming automatically to attention Garner smiled, "Fine sir. And am I pleased to see you".

Chapter 20

After the introductions, Tom, the girls, and Dougal, were led away together with all the senior personnel except the Colonel and Garner, who went as per the Colonel's invitation, down three levels and through a series of corridors, and then finally into a large office.

The Colonel, Humphrey Le Grazie, invited Garner to sit opposite him at the huge desk.

During his army career, and in particular as a sergeant in the Middle East, Garner had served under the Colonel when he was a Major, and they had shared a few missions together and both men had respect for each other as comrades and fighting men.

The Colonel brought Garner up to date, informing him of how the military authorities had finally got together and were organizing powerful groups throughout the UK.

These groups included a few surviving Ministers and government people, and Scientists.

The plan was to eradicate the "Crazies" and the "uncontrollables" as mercifully as possible and bring law and order to the whole country.

But the solution to the virus was paramount and work had started on an answer but was still no nearer to being discovered.

Garner interrupted the Colonel here and stood up to get his satchel bag that he had put on a chair by the door when they had first walked in.

He returned to the desk, taking from the satchel the file of papers and the sample that he had taken from the safe at Squires Manor.

"Here, sir. I was advised to pass this information to a suitable organisation" and he handed the items to the Colonel before sitting down again.

Garner then related the story of his days since leaving his home, omitting his incarceration in prison, but emphasising the importance of the events at Squires Manor where he had been entrusted with the papers and the sample.

Leaning forward Garner studied the papers as the Colonel looked slowly through them.

There was a thin file of formulae that to the two men meant absolutely nothing, and that was accompanied by a small glass phial that contained a light yellow liquid.

"Looks like a urine sample to me" chuckled the Colonel as he held it up to the light.

Deciding that the whole package should be studied by the base's sole scientist, the Colonel buzzed through to some exterior control area and asked for certain people to attend his office, "Pronto".

"So, Garner" the Colonel began, "What are your plans now?"

"I'm not really sure, Sir" Garner said, "My main concerns were for my daughter and Lizzie, the nurse, once we had formed a group, then the lad, Tom".

He paused, then, "And my wife. I don't know if she's OK, or where she might be".

The Colonel leant back in his high backed leather seat and peered over his half-moon spectacles.

"Well, why don't you consider resuming your military career and help us?"

He searched Garner's face for a reaction, "We might just discover where your wife is". The Colonel suggested.

Garner had missed his army days and he gladly agreed to help the Colonel and the new movement in their quest to get things back to normal, or as near to what was normal as possible, ensuring that his daughter would be safe and well.

"Good" And both men stood and the Colonel leant across his desk to shake Garner by the hand, "Welcome aboard, Sergeant Garner" he said with a genuine smile on his tanned face.

"I've got a job for you, already" he informed Garner, and went on to inform him of his wish that Garner accompany a Captain Sinclair and a party of armed men, and a few tanks, and return to relieve the naval contingent at the Portland base.

"As you've just come from there I deem that you must have a fair idea on the best approaches, and of course, any possible danger points" the Colonel said.

"Therefore Garner I believe that at present you're the right man for the job. Sinclair is a good man, but I think that it is wise that you assist him in relieving those poor chaps at Portland" the Colonel went on.

Standing sharply to attention Garner snapped a smart salute, and accepted the assignment.

"Good man" the Colonel once again shook Garner's hand vigorously then rang for his aide to bring other officers to the office.

A further briefing followed involving the introduction of Captain Sinclair to Garner, and two other NCO's.

Colonel introduced Garner as the new senior Sergeant, and the Captain and two NCO's welcomed him and shook his hand.

Garner was beginning to feel happier than he had for a long time.

One of the NCO's took him to an upper floor where there was a basic storeroom and Garner was kitted out with military clothing and footwear.

They then went to yet another store where Garner was issued with weaponry.

One of the weapons was new to him.

It was a very powerful stun gun that could stun up to eight persons within a distance of twenty feet of the user.

The result of being hit by this weapon was total coma that lasted for twenty-four hours.

This was to be the weapon to help overcome the "Crazies".

But, and it was a big But, the weapon was not totally proven.

It had some 'teething' problems, and they were expected to be sorted out in the field of service.

For example it required recharging after twenty seconds of continuous use.

At most, as discovered in testing, twenty seconds of power was all that could be currently relied upon.

Finally, and with the help of the NCO, they carried all of his new gear and weaponry to another higher floor where the living quarters were and Garner was shown the room where he was to reside between manoeuvres and patrols.

The room was next to the one allocated to Tom, and opposite a larger room allocated to Sammy and Lizzie.

Later, during the evening, Garner was able to sit with his daughter, Lizzie, and Tom, as they ate in a small canteen deep in the bowels of the complex.

"Now don't be mad" he began to tell Sammy, "But I've joined up again".

The youngster looked immediately perplexed and her mouth hung open.

"Noooooooooooo . . . ." She managed her objection awkwardly.

Gently he explained that now she, Lizzie and Tom, were in a place of safety he felt that he had a duty to help put the country right, using his years of trained experience.

With tears in her big eyes Sammy nodded her agreement and cuddled up to her father.

She realised that it really made sense and felt better when he continued, telling her that he was to be based there with them and go out on 'patrols' now and then.

Tom was to spend time with an eminent doctor at the base who was going to study the extent of his blindness to ascertain if the condition could be reversed.

Dougal, Tom told Garner, had been temporarily adopted by the Colonel's subaltern, a female officer, and was being spoilt in her private quarters.

Tom had been assured that he would be getting the animal back eventually.

"As it happens I'll be going out on a mission with a group tomorrow morning" Garner told them, "Should'nt be long. Maybe a couple of days".

Sammy began to weep quietly and he embraced her gently kissing the top of her head before standing up to leave.

As he moved towards the canteen entrance he signalled for Lizzie to follow him out into the corridor.

Lizzie got up from her seat and obediently followed Garner outside.

"Look after Sam for me" said, facing her.

"Of course I will" Lizzie smiled, "I promise", and she surprised him by suddenly hugging him, and looking up into his eyes she said, "You take care, do you hear?" and she kissed his cheek.

Something made him pull her back as she drew away and he held her in a close embrace and kissed her purposefully on the lips.

Then, as if embarrassed, Garner quickly turned and marched swiftly down the corridor to the lifts.

Lizzie was completely taken aback and watched with her mouth open as he disappeared into one of the lifts.

With a smile on her face she returned to sit beside Sammy and she put her arm around the youngster.

"Your Dad will be fine. You'll see. He'll be back in no time" and taking a tissue from her pocket she gently wiped the tears from Sammy's cheeks.

That night Garner slept in an upper dormitory with the two NCO's and Captain Sinclair.

The Captain was a slightly built man, aged about thirty, with jet black hair and a thin face.

Although moustaches had not been officers' fashion for many years Captain Sinclair sported a thin wispy line of hair above his top lip.

This tended to make him look a little weak, but those that knew him, knew different.

Raul Sinclair came from a middle class family, all now dead, and he had worked his way up from the lowly rank of Private to become a well respected and loved officer, gaining distinction and medals while in the Middle East and Afghanistan.

The night soon passed and they were awakened the following morning at five o'clock.

After a full breakfast Garner went with Sinclair up the lift and out into the vast flat compound area that was now busy with trucks and two tanks.

Fully equipped Garner climbed aboard the leading truck and sat next to Captain Sinclair.

The Captain spoke quietly in a hand held radio, "OK, gentlemen. Let's away".

One of the tanks drove first out of the large security gates with Garner's truck behind.

They were followed by three other trucks, all carrying fully armed troops wearing newly designed overalls to protect them from any close contact with 'sick' people.

And finally the second tank rolled out as the 'tail-end-charlie' of the convoy.

The convoy moved South along desolate country roads, by-passing large towns where possible.

At a steady pace the vehicles swept towards it's destination.

Sinclair, who commanded the convoy, consulted his watch.

"We should arrive there at 1200 hours" he informed Garner.

The two men began to relax with each other and they began to chat as their driver remained quiet and kept at a regular twenty yards behind the tank.

The convoy passed through dead villages, driving along deserted 'B' roads and some winding lanes.

Flocks of birds, like the animals that Garner had seen on his travels, untouched by the virus that had decimated the humans, surged wildly into the air as the tank travelling at point disturbed them in the tall trees that grew beside the lanes.

"I gather that you and Colonel Le Grazie served together in Iraq and Afghanistan?" Sinclair" said as he and Garner talked.

"Yes. I did a few special missions with the Colonel, but he was just Major Le Grazie then" Garner told him.

"Special Missions?" the Captain raised an eyebrow.

Garner smiled, "Yes. It's no secret now, after all who's going to worry about it, but we were both serving in the SAS then".

"Oh" came the reply, "You were one of those scoundrels, were you?" and he grinned.

He thinks highly of you, you know". Sinclair continued, "I'm sure that he is over the bloody moon now that you're back with us".

Garner felt comfortable with the Captain and they swapped stories of their respective careers, finding out a little of their army days, and their private lives.

Garner discovered that, like himself, Sinclair had been unlucky with his personal life, and he had split with his wife just a month before the virus hit the UK.

Within three weeks his wife and their two young sons were dead. Victims of the virus.

Garner noticed the tearful eyes as the Captain turned his face away and their conversation ended.

It was duly quiet in the cab from then on until the convoy approached the hilly back roads that led up to the main gates of the Portland Naval Base.

The convoy halted and making sure that it was clear to leave the truck Garner jumped down from the cab and quickly entered the guardhouse situated beside the open gates.

The gates were not just open but had been severely damaged and forced, completely destroying them as initial security to the base.

There was nobody in the guardhouse but Garner found that the communications to the main administration building were still functioning although the inside of the gatehouse complex had been trashed.

He got through to an officer who brought a very tired but delighted Commander Richards to the phone.

"Garner, old chap. Ai'nt I glad to hear your voice" the Commander greeted Garner, "come on in, by all means, old chap. And bring all of your friends".

He then gave Garner instructions as to where they were to bring the convoy, and where they were to disgorge all of the men, weaponry, and other welcome supplies.

Later, after the men had been sent to various strategic positions, Garner and Captain Sinclair sat together with Commander Richards, and CPO Patterson, and the Commander brought them up to date.

The "Crazies", the mob that Garner had reported as he had flown over them in the helicopter, had indeed attempted to attack the base again, and this time had almost been successful in gaining entry into the main building, but had been courageously repulsed by the small band of naval ratings there.

There had been many fatalities within the attackers before they had ran baying madly from the scene, and back towards the old fort.

It was there that the "Crazies" were thought to amass before their sorties at the base.

Commander Richards voice faltered as he then went on to tell them that they had lost four ratings killed.

One of them, a twenty-three year old Wren had stayed at her post at one of the vulnerable doorways, firing at the invaders with her automatic weapon.

She had continued to fire on them, killing many and scaring the remainder off, although mortally wounded herself.

CPO Patterson had reached her just in time to see the attackers disappearing, and then as he had sat beside her, cradling her in his arms, she had died.

Commander Richards was in obvious need of rest and Captain Sinclair informed him that they were there to take over and relieve him of his duties.

Sinclair went on to commend the Commander and told him that he and his remaining command would be taken back to the base in Dorset by Garner and a small squad the following day.

Sinclair felt that now with their superior weaponry and substantial manpower, and with the firepower of the strategically placed tanks, he would comfortably be able to hold the Naval Base until a fleet made up of British and American war ships arrived in about two week's time.

The fleet had luckily been at sea, in vast oceans, when the deadly epidemic had spread throughout the world.

Sinclair continued by telling them that Portland would then be a powerful Southern base for them to work from providing the virus and the "Crazies" were kept at bay.

That night all was quiet and they rested, sharing a few glasses of the Commander's Scotch, before retiring to sleep.

Garner, and the party that he was to escort back to the Dorset base, were scheduled to be woken at six the next morning, but as it became light at about five-thirty, the base was again attacked.

"Bloody Crazies" CPO Patterson retorted, "When are they ever going to give up?"

This time the strength was totally on the side of Sinclair and his men but it made it difficult for Garner to leave just yet.

He considered his chances, then, with gunfire going on all around the docks Garner told Sinclair that it probably was a good time to go, whilst the main group of attackers were spread around the area.

"I agree" Sinclair said, "Get your people aboard the trucks and hurry out of here. Do not stop for anything, you hear?"

Wishing each other 'Good Luck', the two men shook hands and parted, Sinclair going directly to support his men fending off the larger of the attacking force.

Garner, his two other NCO's, and twelve other ranks, quickly loaded the Naval group onto the three trucks and then they raced along the quayside and out into the surrounding streets.

Turning a corner they screeched to a halt as they became faced with a mass of screaming and baying "Crazies".

"Bloody 'ell. There must be 'undreds of the bastards" Garner's driver exclaimed.

It was pitiful to see men and, in particular, women of all ages, affected by the madness and acting in this ghastly way, and looking totally demented.

The throng surged forward, brandishing all kinds of implements as weapons.

One man even held a long pointed pole that had a human head spiked on top.

As the mass of "Crazies" hurtled towards them Garner ordered the NCO driving his truck to drive through them.

"You mean run 'em down, sarge?" the soldier asked incredulously.

"Yeah. That's what I mean. Bowl the buggers over. Go right through them. Like a knife through butter, son. Go" Garner replied, an evil grin on his face.

The driver floored the accelerator and released the clutch and the truck shuddered then screeched off like a rocket, crashing through the mass of human figures.

Garner leant out of the cab window and fired a sub machine gun at those who attempted to cling on to the vehicle; another soldier did the same on the other side of the truck.

Bodies were mashed under the truck as it sped through the mob, and the troops in the back of the truck sprayed the "Crazies" with bullets as they drove away.

Horrible screams of agony were mixed with those of the insane attackers alongside.

The following truck also raced through, following their lead, but the third truck halted as the driver was severely injured by a blast from an old shotgun that one of the "Crazies" used as the truck came alongside the remainder of the mob.

Within moments a mass of crazed humans had climbed all over the truck and amid the frantic shooting the escorting personnel and some of the naval ratings were horribly slain, including CPO Patterson.

He was seen leaping from the truck, his service revolver in his hand, firing at those nearest to him.

Too many bodies engulfed him and he was torn to pieces within seconds by the unnatural strength of the "Crazies".

At a safe distance down the road Garner ordered the driver to stop and he jumped out.

As the following truck eased up behind them he looked back to see that it was of no use trying to rescue anybody in the third truck, and so he decided to continue onwards, back to the safety of the main Dorset base.

Everyone was very quiet on their journey back, particularly Garner who felt somehow guilty for the deaths of the occupants in the third truck.

He spoke just once, ordering that Captain Sinclair be informed by radio of the loss of the personnel in the third truck due to the ghastly events outside of the Portland base.

All were very relieved upon approaching the base, and after the gates had been closed behind them, and they disbanded, Garner spent a few minutes speaking with Commander

Richards, his sympathetic words attempting to console a very upset officer for the loss of some of his men, and in particular CPO Patterson, who was not just a lower rank sailor, but a friend of many years.

Commander Richards drew himself upright and saluted Garner then shook his hand.

"You did your best for all of us, and for myself and my men I thank you. It was not your fault that the CPO and the others died. Good Luck", and with tears in his eyes the Commander turned and followed his men into the main complex.

Garner followed them into the building and then down in the lift to the floor where Colonel Le Grazie's office was.

As he walked down the corridor his mind worked overtime, composing a report in his head, defining clearly all of the recent events.

Feeling quite mentally exhausted Garner rapped on the door to the Colonel's office.

"Enter" he heard the precise clear-cut voice of the senior officer.

Garner opened the door and entered the office.

The Colonel sat behind his desk and Garner saw the ramrod back of a man standing and facing the Colonel.

A cold sweat and an intense hatred flushed through him as the man turned to face him, his cruel face grinning, his deep black eyes penetrating.

"Hello, Ron, old man. How the devil are you . . . ?" Harvey Rollison said.

Garner exploded with rage, and raised his sub machine gun to bear on this man . . . .

Chapter 21

"Sergeant Garner!!" The loud authoritative and clear sharp tone of the Colonel's voice brought him to his senses and, clenching his teeth, he lowered the weapon and snapped to attention, facing his superior officer across the desk.

"Now. Put that thing down and pull yourself together. Good God, man, I knew that there was something between you and Corporal Rollison, but I was not aware it had got to this level" the Colonel continued, "When we were together in Iraq you two were my best pair. What on earth has changed you?"

"I'd rather not say, sir" Garner replied shortly, still standing stiffly before the desk.

"At ease, man. Relax" the Colonel ordered Garner then turned to Rollison.

"And you, Rollison. What have you to say about this?"

"Nothing, sir" Rollison said.

He hesitated, and then continued, "We fell out after leaving the army, sir. A private thing, sir"

"Well. Consider yourselves back and under my command for the duration. Forget your differences, or at least keep them in check and out of my sight and sound. As long as you work for and with me, as you once did very well, that is all I ask"

The Colonel was standing and he looked hard at each of them in turn.

"Right?" he demanded his voice strong and concise.

Both men, standing side by side just two feet apart, raised themselves upright and, staring directly past the Colonel's head, replied, "Yes, sir!"

They were then ordered to sit down in the two chairs facing the Colonel and for the following two and a half hours the Colonel discussed his plans for them and a team of 'special' soldiers that they were to select and train.

Although Garner had bad feelings for Harvey Rollison he knew how good he was to have on the team, so suppressing the intense anger and suspicion he had of the man he resigned himself to going along with the Colonel's wishes, knowing that he could be such an important part of the team that might begin to make life as normal as possible again.

In Rollison's case he was quite happy to enjoy the luxuries offered by being fed and watered and cared for by expert medics, and he would patiently bide his time to get rid of Garner, after getting from him what he thought was his, and would set him up for life.

This showed the state of the man's mind considering that while the whole country was in such an uncontrolled and unpoliced situation, there were many opportunities for the plunder of many and very valuable riches from unprotected locations.

Rollison was obsessed with regaining something that he thought Garner had, and Garner had no idea of this.

After the two men had left, one by one, as the Colonel had purposefully kept Rollison back so that there was little chance of them staring a fight out in the corridor, the Colonel sat and mused over the situation, remembering that although they had been quite close at the beginning of their term in Afghanistan, he had seen a gradual rift occurring between them that had caused some concern with the young lieutenant who had led them at the time.

It had not affected their records and they had continued to fight and act as professional soldiers as they had always done.

The Colonel had been quite surprised to learn of both men resigning and leaving the force when they arrived back in the UK.

He had since been posted to another depot at the time and had learned of it later, and had felt somewhat disappointed as the army was losing two very good experienced soldiers.

So now the Colonel had to concentrate on the way ahead and he sat planning their duties for the following days.

Major Havering was called into the office to work with the Colonel who wanted the two newcomers guided by a more senior type.

The Major was brought up to date with the history of Garner and Rollison and he looked forward to working with them.

The selection and training of the new 'Probing and Housekeeping' group began the following day and it went well.

The major allowed the two NCO's to work closely together, watching for any break in their association that could threaten the ultimate plan.

Garner found himself getting used to the situation and he kept control of himself, working with Rollison just like in their old days together, concentrating hard to make a successful formation required to go out in the field and begin to bring some kind of control and order to the few unaffected population in the area.

Evenings were spent with Sammy and sometimes with Lizzie as well, although as she was a nurse she had been given duties in the small but well equipped hospital section lower down in the complex.

Both girls had noticed how Garner had become quiet and brooding at first but after some days he began to lighten up whilst in their company.

Sammy had intimated in her way that she did not like 'Uncle' Harvey being there, and had seemed very surprised when he had suddenly appeared.

He had been friendly to the youngster, but Sammy naturally did not like him.

She remembered that her mother had gone off with him for a while when she was younger, and seeing him again unsettled her for a while.

The following few weeks were given to intensive training with the newly formed group, which included using and becoming used to some new weaponry.

There were a few changes made as some of the original chosen men were found not to be to the standard required, and were subsequently replaced by personnel, some female, who volunteered for the important duties planned.

Eventually Major Havering reported to the Colonel that Garner and Rollison had formed a very good squad of fifty, and that the squad was ready to initiate it's roll out in the field.

The members of the new group were made up from all three major services, and a few civilians, including a couple of firemen and a policeman.

One of the men, a hard ex-marine by the name of Collins, became a close cohort of Rollison's and Garner felt that he would have to watch them closely, suspecting some plot that his old adversary may be planning.

Something illegal, or immoral.

The others had proven themselves very reliable in the use of weaponry and had worked well out on the assault course.

So now they were all ready and waiting for orders for their first assignment.

The following weeks were to prove dangerous, interesting, and sad, and some of the group would die.

Garner knew this, and he resolved again to survive and return to his daughter.

But Rollison had other ideas.

Chapter 22

Following weeks of intensive training, and getting the small army of men to 'gel' there then followed some weeks of patrolling during which they came across a few groups of 'organised' "Crazies", and just one small family of normal, and as yet unaffected people.

The "Crazies" had been mercifully eradicated.

This had upset two of the newly formed group, and they were allowed to drop out.

Nobody was forced into the unholy task of slaying the unfortunate "Crazies".

Their very first day out on patrol took them North to the nearest village where they found no evidence of human life at all.

The day was overcast and there had been a fine drizzle of rain causing a general dampness among the patrol and prompting them to don their wet weather overalls.

Upon entering the village they fully expected to find a few rotting corpses at least but were surprised to discover absolutely nothing but a pack of wild dogs.

Over the preceding weeks these once loyal domestic animals had now grouped and were running together with two German Shepherd dogs that appeared to be the pack's leaders.

There were nine of them, ranging from the big German Shepherds down to a small Jack Russell.

In between there were a range of mixed mongrels.

The patrol had split into two groups with Garner leading five men to one end of the village, on a house to house search, and Rollison taking four others in the opposite direction.

Garner's group heard shots from the direction that the others had taken and they ran fast to back them up, expecting a confrontation with the "Crazies", or some other threat.

Turning into an alley that led to an area of waste ground, walled around on three sides, Garner and his men came upon Rollison taking his time and callously shooting the dogs as they scrambled in terror, trapped in a corner.

Before Garner could intervene Rollison had finished off the majority of the animals, his final shot only wounding the small Jack Russell, causing it to scream in agony.

White faced and raging at Rollison, Garner ordered him to stop shooting and he walked over to the poor animal and dispatched it quickly with one shot from his Browning side arm.

The men were aware of the bad feeling between Garner and Rollison and now witnessed the sergeants as he commanded them to continue their scheduled orders and check out every possible corner of the village where someone could exist, whether they be 'normal' or "Crazie".

An hour later and satisfied that there was no human to assist or to take back with them the group drove out of the village and moved towards some farmland a few miles further North.

They checked a large farm and discovered a few dead animals, cattle and pigs, whose rotting corpses, now rancid with the smell of decaying flesh, were being enjoyed by swarms of huge bluebottle flies.

With no reason to stay, Garner and the patrol drove on to a small group of cottages further up the grassy slopes.

Probably built centuries ago for the farm labourers these small buildings had been regularly maintained and looked inviting.

Driving their two army trucks up to the front of the row of cottages they halted and leapt from the vehicles to commence their search.

Before Garner could issue any commands they were suddenly attacked by a mob of screaming "Crazies" armed with various tools as weaponry.

This mob had seen them approaching and had stayed hidden until all of the soldiers had alighted from the trucks.

The attack was a complete surprise.

Garner, standing beside his driver, a young Welsh lad, was caught a glancing blow by a "Crazie" wielding a pick axe handle and he staggered to one side then fell to the ground.

The Welsh lad stood over Garner, protecting him, and he fired off a few shots from a light machine pistol before he too was felled by a huge "Crazie" who came up from behind and split the lad's head in two using an axe.

From his position on the ground Garner fired his weapon in short bursts, but with geat effect, and together with Rollison and the others they eventually accounted for all of the mob.

After a full count they found the bodies of seventeen people of mixed ages and sex.

Garner instructed two men to carry the Welsh lad's body and, covering it with a blanket; they placed it in the back of Garner's truck.

God! Garner agonized. His first patrol and he had lost a man.

He was to feel bad for some weeks following this black day.

Rollison meanwhile had got his men to drag all of the dead "Crazies" and pile them in the front room of one of the deserted cottages.

He then poured petrol around the room before casually lighting himself one of his black cheroots, drawing in the acrid tobacco taste, then flicking it through the open doorway.

The room erupted in a burst of intense fire and the patrol drove away leaving the small hamlet roaring with fire.

Not a word was spoken as they drove back to base, their thoughts dwelling on the attack and the loss of one of their colleagues.

Upon their return to base all of them were taken through a special room, separated from the main complex, where they showered under a cleansing detergent that was considered to eradicate any germs they may have picked up during the patrol and contact with any sick people.

Their clothing and weaponry was processed in a similar way.

Chapter 23

The experience of losing one of their group was felt badly and it took some days of further reconnoitring before they began to feel more relaxed but sharper in their senses when out on patrol.

It was a cool but sunny day when they met the Lambert family.

The patrol, now with a new and experienced man called Mason replacing the Welsh lad, were driving along a narrow country lane that ran through the bottom of a thickly wooded valley.

Mason, who was driving the lead truck, suddenly spotted movement through some trees to their left, and he told Garner.

The driver also drew to a halt knowing that his patrol leader would want to investigate.

Garner ordered the men to leave the vehicles and to spread out, and they began to climb the wooded slopes in the direction that Mason indicated.

Quietly making their way uphill, through green sun speckled woodland, nothing but the sounds of birds could be heard.

Then came the faint sound that could not have been any known bird.

Everybody stood still.

Listening intently the men heard the clear and unmistakable voice of a young child singing a nursery rhyme.

Leaving Rollison in charge of the patrol Garner took Mason and they crept slowly up to the top and found themselves nearing the singing child.

Garner spotted her first and he put a finger to his lips, instructing Mason to stay silent.

They both now saw the young singer, or "Angel" as she was later to be called by the men, sitting on a fallen tree.

The child, a small curly blonde headed girl aged about five, held a tatty knitted doll out before her and was lost in her rendering of the song, as if singing to the doll.

Garner and Mason now approached the child who upon realising their presence stopped singing.

The two soldiers, smiling at the little girl, were just ten yards from her when a sharp command was heard from within the trees to their left.

"That's far enough. You go near her and you're dead".

The concerned but authoritative voice of a man who continued, "Drop your weapons".

Garner and Mason did so, bending to place the guns in the long grass.

Neither of them could see their adversary.

"Who are you? Where're you from?" a huge man built like a weight lifter, and about six feet, seven inches, came out from behind a tree and the child ran swiftly to him and hugged his legs.

The man brandished a double-barrelled shotgun and he aimed it at them.

"We are from the Southern UK Authority" Garner began, "We are a force intent in the bringing back fully civilised and healthy control to the country".

He went on to explain the patrol's mission and offered to help the man in any way possible.

The man listened in silence.

He was considering that Garner had mentioned a 'patrol', which meant that there were others nearby.

Garner took a step forward.

"Stay right there. I'll shoot!" the man snarled and raised the shotgun, aiming directly at Garner.

"We're here to help . . . ." Garner began.

"And we don't need your help. You've been mixing it with those poor sick souls".

The man shouted, "And we don't want you near. Turn around and clear off. Do anything else and I'll shoot. I mean it" he said.

Then, the man suddenly stiffened, and he lowered the shotgun.

"Now, that's sensible . . . ." Garner heard Rollison's voice, and he and Mason saw that the big Corporal had appeared behind the man and was pressing the muzzle of his light machine gun to the back of the man's head.

For all of his faults Rollison was an experienced and clever soldier.

He had come up silently through the trees to surprise the man from behind.

Rollison's usual colleague Collins now came into view and he took the shotgun from the stricken man.

The little girl still clung to the man's legs, her pretty face turned up and looking at Rollison with an expression of puzzlement.

Garner now approached the man.

"Are you alone?"

The man stood upright. Defiant.

Staring straight ahead, he remained silent.

"Mummy?" the little girl began to cry, quiet little sobs.

"There are others?" Garner asked.

Crouching down the man hugged the girl to him.

He sighed and looking up at Garner he confessed, "Yes. But we are all safe. And more importantly we are all well" he continued.

Standing up now, he lifted the child, holding her gently.

What we don't want is someone coming into our fold and bringing that bloody sickness with them".

The girl clung tightly to him, "Mummy . . . I want Mummy" she cried, tears streaming down her cheeks.

Quietly, and patiently, Garner now explained in greater depth what their mission was.

He told the man of the dangers threatened by the wandering groups of the infected people, and he further informed the man of the International contacts and the work being carried out to produce a vaccine against the sickness.

"We are a well organised and equipped organisation with a safe and secure base, free of any sickness. I trust it. And I have my daughter living there with me" Garner concluded.

Calming the child as he listened to Garner the man relaxed and eventually agreed to lead Garner and his men to the small secluded valley where he and his family had remained hidden for the past few months.

As he walked, with the man carrying the child in front, Garner realised that the man knew very little of those that were called "Crazies", and the terrible fate of anyone caught by them.

They walked single file through thick lush green woodland and down into a steep sided valley.

A stream ran through it with a rough track, wide enough to take a vehicle, that led up to an old stone built cottage.

As they neared the building a woman aged about thirty came out of the door holding another shotgun.

The poor woman looked perplexed as she saw the man with the child leading a group of armed strangers towards her home.

"It's alright, love" the man called out to her, "They're here to help us" and he lowered the child to the ground where she ran swiftly to the woman, crying, "Mummy".

Crouching down to hug the child to her the woman lay the gun on the ground.

The group was led up to the door where Garner gave orders for the patrol to rest and he entered the cottage with the big man.

Rollison ordered two men to take up strategic positions while allowing the remainder to sit about the cottage frontage, chatting and some lighting cigarettes.

Inside the cottage Garner learned of the family's plight.

The big man introduced himself as Maurice Lambert, the owner of the cottage and the land contained by the valley.

He then introduced other members of his family.

Sitting in an old ragged armchair beside the huge inglenook fireplace was Samuel Lambert.

Maurice's brother.

He had a roughly made crutch beside him.

Maurice explained that Samuel was the little girl's father and he and his wife, Lillian, also had a boy aged about eight who was now sitting at his father's feet.

"This is Harry" Maurice smiled as he indicated the boy, bending to ruffle the lad's hair lovingly, "And this little bundle of mischief is our Natalie" and he ruffled her hair as well.

He continued to tell Garner how early on when the virus began to sweep the country he had brought his brother and his family from Dorchester to stay with him.

They had purposefully cut themselves off from civilisation, living off of the land, and here Maurice pointed out a substantial area, or allotment, where he grew various vegetables.

He was also apparently quite astute at trapping rabbits and once he had shot and killed a passing deer.

They'd had no experience, and were completely unaware of the effects that had caused such madness, and the new 'social' groups of insane people that Garner had referred to as "Crazies".

"You know. You'll be much safer with us. We have an extensive medical facility and there is opportunity for education for the children" Garner smiled and motioned towards the youngsters.

After leaving the family to discuss his offer Garner joined his men and relaxed, sitting with his back to the cottage wall, and closing his eyes as he felt the warm sunlight on his face.

Maurice Lambert joined him after a while and informed him of the family's decision.

"We will come with you" Maurice said, "It will be quite a wrench to leave here but I guess that you are right. It makes sense. You've convinced us that it will be safer".

Garner stood and he shook the big man's hand, then he asked Maurice to lead four of the soldiers back to where they had left the trucks, and to bring them to the cottage, through the hidden entrance that they had missed earlier as they drove through the other valley.

Then, after collecting all that they required and packed them into the rear of the trucks, the family boarded the vehicles and were driven off, leaving the cottage behind.

Maurice had locked the cottage up, but that did not guarantee that anyone could not break in.

He felt sad about it but he realised that their lives could be in danger and they were now under the protection of organised and armed friends.

The big man sat beside Garner on the journey back to the base and he told the sergeant that his brother, Samuel, had accidentally hurt his leg quite seriously some weeks before and it was probably fortunate now that he could get proper attention for it.

Garner sensed that Maurice was a good man, of strong character, and he was to encourage him to train and to join the unit during the following weeks.

Natalie, the little girl, soon became a favourite of the staff at the base and she delighted in singing her nursery rhymes.

The men called her their little "Angel".

Chapter 24

It was September now, and the weather had changed drastically.

Torrential rain poured for four continuous days and temperatures plummeted to unseasonable lows.

The constant deluge caused local flooding and rivers burst their banks to add to the misery.

Regular patrols had been postponed, and time was spent continuing to train within the complex and clean weaponry.

Reports had started to come in from bases situated in the North of England of fewer bands of "Crazies", although there were still a number of larger groups in the major cities.

The base's helicopter had flown up to a base near Manchester and upon it's return reported seeing a group of about a dozen "Crazies" out near the Stonehenge area.

Garner was ordered to take his two trucks and his squad and go find this group and, if necessary (and it usually was) eradicate them.

They drove carefully along water covered lanes and roads, sometimes at the foot of slopes driving through deep water.

They were just a few miles from Stonehenge when they spotted a group of people lying together in the lea of a hedge that ran alongside an open field.

The convoy slowed and then halted as Garner told the driver to stop.

Staying in the vehicle he studied the bodies for any sign of movement.

There was none.

"Stay here" he ordered his crew and jumped down from the cab, his automatic weapon at the ready.

Garner slowly approached the group suspecting that it could be a trap.

He had never been able to forget his error the time that they had lost the Welsh lad.

But when only a few yards from them he just knew that all of them were dead, stiffened in rigor mortis.

Garner signalled for the squad to come to him and the men leapt from the two vehicles with their weapons at the ready, leaving the two drivers in the cabs.

The men stood around the scene looking at the obscene figures as they lay in various positions of death. "Don't think we've got a lot to do here, Sarge" Mason said, and he spat in a puddle.

A conversation then took place as to whether they should continue to patrol the area, and Garner was about to order a radio message back to base when one of his crew called out.

"Hey, Sarge. Over here. I think that I heard something" and Garner saw that the man was looking over the hedge and into the field.

Garner joined the man and they both listened intently for a few seconds.

"There. Hear it, Sarge. It seemed to come from over there" the man said and he pointed across the light brown muddy earth to a small Nissen hut-like shelter.

There were many of these shelters dotted across the field and Garner remembered when travelling these roads years ago that this was where pigs were kept.

The shelters were quite small, but big enough to take pigs.

Ordering his men to stay silent he strained to hear what his man had heard.

Yes. There it was.

A plaintiff cry of a girl.

Coming from the shelter nearest to the road.

"Help . . . help me . . . please" came the cry, clearer now.

Garner called over to Rollison, "Stay here with the lads. I'm going to see what's up" and, taking Mason and the soldier who had the keen hearing with him, he led them through a gap in the hedge.

They squelched through the thick slimy quagmire and peered into the dim interior of the shelter.

"Oh, please . . . help me . . . please".

In the darker end of the shelter they saw the form of a person curled up in the foetal position, lying on straw covered in pig dung.

It stank to high heaven and all three men had to take deep breaths of fresh air before they ducked down and reached deep into the void to lift the person out and into the daylight.

It was a girl.

Her long hair was dirty and lank with the mass of dried mud in it.

Her face was filthy but they could see the dark rings of exhaustion around her eyes.

She was of slight build and wore a thick woollen cardigan over a dirty cotton nightdress.

Her legs were bare and streaked with mud.

Mason and the soldier carried her over to the roadway, slipping and sliding awkwardly in the mud.

The girl was laid down on a ground sheet that one of the men quickly got from the back of a truck.

Both her wrists and ankles had been tied tightly with rough sisal rope and after Garner had cut her free with his clasp knife the red and sore skin looked in need of urgent medical attention.

"Thank you" the girl cried, tears streaming down her face.

Most of the men stood well away as Garner and Mason, and the soldier with the keen hearing, crouched beside the girl.

"How did you get into this mess, love?" Garner asked.

The girl spoke quickly, nervously, explaining how only three days ago she had been staying in a caravan with her father when the mob had attacked them at night.

Her father had been dragged away and she did not know where he was or what had become of him.

"Sarge" Mason made Garner aware as the girl began to sit up a bit.

Garner raised his eyebrows.

The girl was very much advanced in pregnancy.

Her belly now huge and obvious as she changed her position on the sheet.

"How long, love?" Garner motioned down at her belly.

She sobbed, "Very soon, I think" she cried.

"How old are you?" Mason asked.

"Nineteen" she replied.

She went on to explain that her fiancé had died two months ago, then her mother, and her father had decided it might be healthier for her at his caravan.

They had driven from North London and had been lucky enough not to experience any meetings with sick groups.

Both men looked each other.

The girl was going to need proper medical attention all round, presupposing that she was totally free from infection.

"Why did they tie me up?" the girl eyed the dead "Crazies".

Garner and Mason did not reply knowing that she was probably meant for eventual slaughter.

"Do you know when, or how they died?" Garner asked the girl.

"I think that it was last night. It was very cold. I noticed that they had been constantly shivering and coughing. They were all soaked through, too" she told them.

"Then this morning I heard some of them moaning and crying and coughing awfully. And then it went quiet. I thought that I was going to die, too. Still tied up in that hut thing" the girl continued.

Garner turned to Mason, "Sounds like they got pneumonia" he said.

Deep inside he wondered if their state of health left them weakened and vulnerable to the dangers of natural colds and flus.

Garner then told the girl that she was to be taken to a place of safety where she would be looked after, and Mason easily picked her up and carried her to the leading truck.

As she was being made as comfortable as possible with heavy army blankets around her, the girl suddenly blurted out, "It was that Nun woman!".

Garner stopped and, startled by her outburst, he asked, "What Nun woman?"

"After Dad was taken away they started to hurt me. I thought that I was going to die.

They were pulling my arms. It really hurt. Then, all of a sudden this mad woman, dressed in dirty black robes, just like a Nun, stopped them and started screaming at them".

Garner was amazed.

It was her again.

The Nun at the cottage, then at Lulworth.

"She pointed at my stomach and stopped them hurting me, then she garbled something . . . . I couldn't understand any of them . . . all the time I was a prisoner, and she made them tie me up and I was carried everywhere"

"Where is she now?" Garner looked back at the dead bodies.

"I don't know. She was around the first day then I never saw her again".

Garner's brain was racing.

How was the Nun travelling?

She seemed to get around very easily.

And it was only because she had seen the girl's pregnancy that she had saved her then.

Garner then ordered the men to don special gloves that had been issued to them and they dragged all of the bodies through the gap in the hedge and piled them together in the field.

Once again it was Rollison who heavily doused the pile with a can of petrol before setting it alight.

The trucks drove away, going back to base as a plume of black smoke rose from the pyre into the leaden skies.

Back at the base Garner made his report and went with his squad to be disinfected and cleansed before taking a few hours rest, spending it with Sammy and Tom, who now had Dougal back.

The girl, her name was Natalie, had been thoroughly examined after a cleansing bath then was put in a quarantined room, and nursed by an elderly matron-like woman who had once been a children's nurse.

Within a week Natalie had given birth to twins, a boy and a girl, and all three were well.

The new mother settled in and became a useful member of the complex, assisting in the canteen.

She named her little boy Ronald, and the little girl Samantha.

But for a long time Garner was deeply puzzled by the ghostly appearances of the mad Nun.

Chapter 25

There was one strange, but quite humorous, incident during a routine patrol to the big town of Dorchester.

This was the hilarious encounter with Samuel "Jolly" Rogers.

The patrol came across Samuel as they turned into the high street of the now deserted town.

The man was coming out of a well-known bank carrying two large suitcases that he had managed to stuff full of banknotes, not all entirely from the bank as it turned out, but he had gained entry to many shops as well during that morning.

But what was most surprising was that Samuel was dressed completely as a circus clown and he had even painted his face and was wearing a large bulbous false red nose.

"What the hell?" Garner gasped as the truck drew up beside a large white van that the clown was loading the cases into.

The four men, sitting behind Garner in the truck, were already laughing.

Garner jumped down from the truck and was met quite amiably by the clown as he approached, introducing himself as he held out one hand.

"So nice to meet you" the clown smiled through the painted smile at Garner, "My name is Samuel Rogers".

The man was obviously in good health.

Smiling, but also with an air of authority, Garner informed the clown that he was now under arrest on the most serious charge of looting, and that he was to be taken into custody there and then.

Rollison, who had got into the back of the van, called Garner to the rear to view the interior.

The van was almost full with boxes and packages of various valuables, including jewellery, cash, and ornaments.

Also there was a stack of circus costumes and paraphernalia.

Still smiling Garner returned to where the clown stood chatting to two men guarding him.

"What on earth do you think you are doing?" he asked, "What good is all that to you?"

"Well" began Samuel, "The way I see it is that all of this is just laying around, waiting to be taken, and I think that there may come a day when it could be of great use to me" and he chuckled, an infectious chuckle that made his guards laugh.

"After all, if I or anybody else don't take it, it will maybe rot or just disappear as everything starts to crumble through lack of use"

A feeble excuse, Garner thought, but he sensed that the poor chap was somewhat safe and not really doing any harm, and that due to constant loneliness he had been affected a bit mentally.

Generally Samuel was harmless, but needed to be taken into care.

The man spoke so sincerely, but with a definite twinkle in his eyes, that all those standing near chuckled too, some actually believing him.

Garner removed a number of very expensive rings, necklaces, and watches that Samuel was wearing over his clown's costume, before having him put in the back of a truck together with his guards.

The clown was quite a jolly and likeable rogue, and his jocular manner was infectious, and Garner and the others were soon enjoying his company, and there was a lot of laughter amongst the men as the trucks made their way back to base.

The van laden with Samuel's forbidden treasure was being driven behind by Rollison and his crony Collins.

On a serious note Rogers did confide to Garner that he had a nasty experience with a group of very 'sick' people just a few days before.

Apparently he had wandered into their midst as they sat gorging themselves on rotten meats inside a store.

They had not attacked and after eyeing him strangely they had seemed to accept him as one of them, offering him some of the rancid flesh.

Rogers had pretended to eat some of the disgusting meat and he had almost vomited before he managed to creep away as they slept, and he had got as many miles as possible between him and them during that night.

Due to the laughter brought on by remarks and the antics of Samuel Rogers no one missed the van until they neared the gates to the base.

Garner was about to order that they turn around and go looking for the missing van when it came haring up fast to meet them.

Rollison apologised but explained that Collins had desperately required to relieve himself and so he had stopped for him.

Garner suspected that the two men had quickly dumped some of the valuables where they could find it later, but there was no way that he could prove it.

Aside from this he had an idea for their entrance into the base and they stopped just out of sight of the gates to prepare for the planned entry.

Colonel Le Grazie watched the returning vehicles on the special CCTV system piped through to his office and he was astonished, but he smiled widely, as he saw the men, including Garner, all dressed as circus clowns and wearing false noses and bright make-up, alighting from the trucks.

The van followed them into the compound.

It was his laughter began to subside that the Colonel suddenly felt a bit feverish, and a slight headache began.

Chapter 26

By the time that Garner had reported the day's events to the Colonel he had showered then had changed into his normal fatigues.

"What was that all about?" the Colonel asked Garner with a smile.

Standing at attention before his senior officer Garner gave his report on their recent patrol into Dorchester and he explained all that there was to know regarding Samuel Rogers, and the beneficial effect that the man had on the troops.

Colonel Le Grazie stood and turning his back on Garner he stifled a fit of laughter.

Garner saw the Colonel's shoulders shaking and guessed that he was enjoying the imagined situation.

Then, turning to face Garner the Colonel forced himself to become properly serious and he ordered his sergeant to fall out, make out the usual written report, then stand down for the day.

Although under arrest Samuel was not incarcerated in any way and following a thorough health check he was free to mingle with the occupants at the base, becoming a source of continuous laughter and fun.

Over the following days Garner and other staff close to the Colonel noticed that each time they faced him he appeared to be suffering from the beginnings of a severe cold.

The Colonel's odd actions had also come under scrutiny and he was eventually ordered by those few in a higher level of command, to allow the medical team to check him over.

Blood tests followed and it was discovered that the Colonel had the initial stage of the virus, and the leading medical expert at the base, Professor Liam Murdoch, decided to try out the incomplete and untested vaccine on him.

It was explained to the Colonel that there was no guarantee that the test vaccine would be successful, but he bravely chose to allow them to go ahead and inject the serum into his arm.

He attempted to continue with some of his duties but he became too ill and was coaxed by the Professor and Garner to rest in the isolation ward, in the medical wing.

The Colonel was a very popular officer and a few friends and colleagues were allowed to visit him, as long as they were wearing the appropriate sterile clothing.

Garner had just made a short visit to see the Colonel and was talking to Professor Murdoch outside in the corridor, discussing the possibilities of how the Colonel had caught the virus, when the poor man suddenly came crashing past them, racing away along the corridor with his gown swirling about his naked body.

Normally the sight of the Colonel bare buttocks would have been hilarious, but Garner and the Professor were now extremely concerned and they sped off after him.

Realising the state of the Colonel's infected mind they attempted to capture him before he had managed to pass his illness on to others in the immediate vicinity.

Cackling and jibbering insanely the Colonel beat his pursuers to his office and he dashed behind his desk and slammed down into his large leather swivel chair.

Garner and Professor Murdoch entered the office just in time to see the Colonel take his service revolver from a drawer of his desk, and deliberately slide the safety catch to 'off'.

"Noooo . . . ." pleaded Garner, who realised the Colonel's intentions.

But he was too late as the Colonel brought the revolver up to his head, laughed out loud, and then shot himself through the mouth.

It was all in slow motion and seemed surreal to Professor Murdoch, who upon seeing the wall behind the Colonel suddenly splattered with brains and blood, realised the horror of it all and he staggered out into the corridor, and he vomited violently against the wall.

The base police, wearing the traditional red band on their caps, came rushing in from all directions and were kept away from the Colonel's body by Garner who warned them of the dangers of infection from the still warm body.

Realising that nobody was safe and that the Colonel must have been affected by some of those who had been brought in recently and interrogated by him, an instant and total quarantine took place within the complex and everyone was tested for the virus.

A young married couple, who together with their baby son had been picked up by a patrol a week before, were found to be 'carriers' and as a small family they were then isolated in a separate building that was sited just outside the perimeter fence of the compound, and were given supplies to live on.

How they had been missed at their admission in the first place was subject to an investigation.

They were told that the Professor and his team would regularly visit them, wearing protective clothing, and there would be an attempt to find a way to 'cleanse' them before allowing them to return as residents at the base.

But even in their new temporary home the couple were not safe and two nights later they were slain by a passing group of three "Crazies" who took the child with them, only to be killed later for food.

A small force was sent out to find and eradicate the murderers when Professor discovered the remains of the young couple, and the patrol that found them, hiding in thick shrubland, quickly ended their days with bursts of automatic weapon fire.

The Colonel was succeeded by an army officer known to Garner and the others.

Major Johnnie Havering, a rather nervous but very experienced officer was to become a good friend of Garner's and Sammy.

The first thing that the Major did was to organise a tighter and totally foolproof method of checking absolutely everyone and everything that entered the complex, even every man, woman or child that came back from or with a patrol.

Like Colonel Le Grazie, the Major had to report to the Group that ruled the complex, a band of senior military personnel and a few surviving government ministers.

Now with a few important changes put in place by the Major, Garner resumed his leadership of regular patrols, while Liam Murdoch researched a viral solution to the terrible plague that still threatened everyone.

Chapter 27

At thirty-nine Liam Murdoch had many years' experience in the study of viral infections and had been fully involved in the intense study and research of the epidemic germ at London University when it all began.

Many of his colleagues had perished in those first terrible weeks as the virus swept through Europe, leaving him in the unenviable position of being a sole expert in the UK.

Quickly escorted out of London by a small force of military personnel, Liam was taken to the complex in Dorset where he was faced by the few people left in authority and given the task of continuing his work to find, initially a deterrent, and ultimately a complete cure.

Now, and with the help of Lizzie, whose medical background would be of assistance, Professor Murdoch spent many long hours in the small laboratory with her.

Liam Murdoch was not your expected boffin type.

Dark haired and with clean cut features and aquiline nose, he was not unattractive to the opposite sex, but apart from his regular sessions in the gym where he kept himself fit and athletic, he was totally committed to his work.

There had been regular radio contact with an organised group in Switzerland, the United States, and Canada, and co-operation between them and Professor Murdoch strived to discover the beginnings of an antidote to the virus.

The Professor was in fact someways towards this and although there had been the disappointment with the treatment to Colonel Le Grazie, he felt that he was making headway.

And during the reading of a patrol report made out by Sergeant Garner he had been very interested in the soldiers comment about a group of "Crazies" who may have died suddenly through contracting pneumonia?

Privately he wondered if it was possible that mother nature would make some amendments by naturally eradicating the insanely sick with man's oldest illness, colds and normal influenza, leading to double pneumonia attacking an already weakened body.

The information and the sample that Garner had brought from Squires Manor had been very useful but, and the Professor was sure of this, the final essential ingredient was yet to be included.

During their regular 'family' hours together Garner found that his daughter and Lizzie got on very well.

Lizzie seemed particularly happy now that her wound had healed and she was enjoying her work assisting 'Liam' as she called him.

Garner now found that he had mixed feelings about this, and was surprised that deep down he was probably jealous of Liam Murdoch.

He had tried to remain distant and had stopped himself from getting too close to the attractive nurse.

Feeling somewhat confused Garner thought, rightly or wrongly, that any feelings for her might affect his resolve to get through this period of emergency.

Anyway, the bad experience he had with his wife had caused him to build a wall about himself that only Sammy could get through.

Lately he had become more confused and had even discovered that he felt frightened that Lizzie might fall for the Professor with whom she was spending so much of her time with.

But, and Garner had no idea of this, all that the Professor was interested in was 'the final and absolute solution' to the epidemic, and the Sergeant had no reason to worry that any romance between the Professor and Lizzie might be a possibility.

With these mixed feelings haunting him Garner now found that during patrols, and off duty, Rollison was becoming more of a menace.

The old bad feelings between them now began again, particularly since their old mentor, the Colonel, was dead.

Rollison attempted many times to undermine Garner's authority and he cause problems whilst out on patrol, sometimes causing resentment and confusion among the men.

Very often Rollison began to use the imaginary situation of the Professor and Lizzie being lovers and he goaded Garner with lurid suggestions that fired the Sergeants temper up and he had to be restrained by Corporal Mason and other loyal men in the group.

Rollison was fast running out of friends, even the despicable Collins now kept out of his way, seeking new friends elsewhere.

It was following a vicious tirade from Rollison one evening in the mess that Major Havering had to intervene and he ordered the Corporal to be suspended from duty and to be kept under guard in his quarters pending further investigations for his disrupting actions.

Garner had returned later to his own quarters and Sammy came in to console her father having been witness to his distress and anger.

In her sweet way Sammy tried to convince Garner that Lizzie was fine and that the nurse was OK with him.

It was not easy for the youngster with her disability but somehow her feelings and the subtle message got through, and after embracing his daughter, Garner kissed the girl's forehead and told her that he understood and that she had made him feel much better.

During the time that they had been at the complex Garner, Sammy and Lizzie had become a small unit together at the evening off duty breaks, and with Tom and the dog Dougal, many happy hours ensued.

But things were about to change.

Chapter 28

It happened all too soon.

In fact it was just two days after the incident had occurred when Rollison had been suspended.

Garner's patrol had just returned.

It was late afternoon.

The sergeant was alone in his quarters, writing his patrol report.

Rollison, still under guard in his quarters, had become angry and frustrated at his incarceration.

It happened that it was his old croney Collins who had been assigned duty to guard him this afternoon and he being not such a diligent soldier had crept into a storeroom opposite the prisoner's room to have a quick cigarette.

Rollison had left the door to his quarters ajar and he knew that Collins had stepped across the corridor to the store.

Grinning evilly, as only he could, Rollison left his room and crossed to the storeroom door where, peering through the small square window, he saw Collins squatting on a low stool reading a magazine and with a cigarette dangling from his lips.

Glancing down Rollison noticed that the key to the storeroom had been conveniently left in the lock by Collins, or someone else, but that did not matter for Rollison slowly and quietly turned it, locking his guard in.

Collins continued to smoke, turning the pages of the magazine, as Rollison walked casually away down the corridor, then around a corner that led to the laboratory area.

Due to it's function the laboratory had to, by design and law, have a separate safety exit to the outside, and Rollison knew this.

He intended to desert.

He'd had enough of these 'pansies'.

He sneered at the thought of his recent comrades.

His bit of business with Garner could wait.

After all he could easily pick up the small hoard of stolen treasures that he and Collins had stowed inside a hollow tree.

Keep it all for himself.

Serves that stupid bastard Collins right!

Quietly entering the laboratory Rollison listened for any sign of activity.

It appeared that the room was empty.

He was alone.

Making his way between the test benches he began his escape, passing areas of test data and equipment, proceeding towards the door marked "Emergency Exit".

Then, he froze in his tracks.

Humming softly to herself Lizzie appeared from the laboratory store carrying in her arms boxes of test items required for the next stage of Professor Murdoch's research.

Suddenly she came face to face with the big Corporal.

Her eyes widened and she gasped, "What are you doing here?" she exclaimed fearfully.

He scared her.

The crazy look in his yellow eyes and the wicked smile turned her legs to jelly.

She trembled as he drew nearer to her.

"I'm out of here" he chuckled, "But I might as well take advantage of a lovely bit of skirt like you, Eh?"

Lizzie started to scream and she dropped the packages.

"Oh yeah" Rollison drooled, licking his thick lips, "What you might call a bonus for all the good work I've done here" and laughing he grabbed her by the shoulders.

Lizzie finally got a piercing scream out as he gripped her throat with one huge hand, forcing the scream to die and bending her across a bench so that it felt as if her spine was about to snap.

She gripped his wrists with both hands, and tried to struggle, cry hoarsely, but he was too strong for her.

Rollison ripped her uniform open at the front, tearing it open easily by the force of his depraved attack.

He slapped her hard, splitting her lip, and forced her down to the floor, grabbing at the hem of her uniform and pulling it upwards.

Outside Sammy and Tom were approaching the laboratory area, strolling along the corridor as they took Dougal for a short exercise before tea.

The little dog was the first to sense the commotion in the laboratory and it began to yap excitedly, pulling at the leash that Tom held.

The blind lad stopped and cocked his head to the side as he listened intently.

He could just about hear Lizzies's cries of anguish from within the laboratory area.

Sammy noticed Tom's distress then heard the cries as well.

Tom faced her and motioned urgently towards the sounds.

Both youngster's went cautiously into the laboratory together, holding hands.

Then suddenly faced with the scene before her, Sammy shrieked out with one of her unique strangled screams, and she staggered against the wall.

Rollison was crouched over Lizzie when he became aware of the interlopers and he rose up, snarling angrily and with a wild look of pure hatred on his cruel face.

Again Sammy shrieked in the strange strangled way, louder this time, and Tom turned away, groping for the doorway in an attempt to get help.

He had no idea of what was actually going on but he just knew that someone was in dire trouble.

Quick as a flash Rollison took a large glass bowl from the bench nearest him and he threw it at the lad, hitting him squarely on the back of the head.

The heavy bowl smashed with the velocity and such was the force of the throw that Tom was instantly felled, toppling silently to the floor.

Lizzie, terrified and now with her mouth uncovered, screamed a piercing screech, and Rollison punched her hard in the face.

Cowering against the wall Sammy was petrified and frozen with fear, staring with wide eyes down at the inert form of Tom, blood flowing freely from a wound in his scalp.

Suddenly Garner stepped into the laboratory.

Having finished his report he had decided to try and see Lizzie alone and tell her of his feelings for her, and he had arrived just in time.

Seeing what Rollison had done to the nurse and fearing the worse, and seeing the state of his daughter, and the injured Tom on the floor, Garner went berserk.

He flew at Rollison who skilfully sidestepped and gave the Sergeant a nasty chop to the back of the neck as he rushed past.

Garner crashed to the floor beside Lizzie who lay crying in fear as Rollison again loomed over her.

Garner bounced up and swung a punch at his adversary, catching him on the side of the jaw.

Rollison fell back and he kicked out as Garner came at him again.

The Sergeant stopped in his tracks as Rollison's boot caught him hard in the crotch.

The pain, and the tears in his eyes, caused him to hesitate.

Rollison leapt at him and head butted him full in the face, breaking his nose for the third time in his life.

Garner, now totally out of it, fell to his knees, blood streaming from his fractured nose.

With that evil grin on his face Rollison picked up another very large glass bowl and was about to smash it over Garner's head when two duty redcaps raced in, having heard the screams and the commotion along the corridors.

"What the hell . . . ?" the leading redcap began, and he saw, just in time, that Rollison had thrown the bowl at him and his companion.

They both ducked to avoid the missile and Rollison took advantage to leap through the emergency exit and race up the stairway, taking three steps at a time.

One of the redcaps stayed with Garner and Lizzie, as the remaining redcap, accompanied by two more who had appeared, chased Rollison up the stairs.

But the Corporal made it outside quickly and he slid through a hidden gap in the compound fencing that he had prepared in readiness for his defection some weeks before.

By the time the redcaps got to the fence and had discovered the gap, Rollison was speeding away on a motorbike that he hidden nearby in thick bushes.

From that first time he had entered the complex the sly Corporal had always planned to leave when it suited him, and he had prepared his escape route well.

Returning to the laboratory the redcaps found other duty officers there, and the Professor.

Sergeant Garner was in a bit of a state, to say the least.

He felt awful.

His face throbbed, and the pain in his groin convinced him that he would never again be able to father a child.

Leaving the Professor, and Major Havering who had been called to the 'crime scene', to check the laboratory and the very important tests on-going therein, Garner, Lizzie, and the youngsters were taken to the hospital wing, Tom being carried on a stretcher, where their wounds were attended to.

Tom was the most seriously injured and he would remain in a coma for some very worrying days.

But this injury was the beginning of a period when the boy's sight began to return, very slowly at first, and totally as time past.

Lizzie, and to a certain extent Sammy, were given sedatives to ease their shock.

Sitting face to face in an ante room later Garner and Lizzie smiled at each other.

He had a broken nose and two black eyes, and she had a fat lip and one black eye.

They smiled again, their smiles turning to laughter and they ended up sobbing with relief in each other's arms.

During an earlier confrontation Rollison had goaded Garner as usual and on this occasion made reference to him having taken Garner's wife easily.

Rollison now believed that the stupid woman must have got hold of the very thing that he had always searched for.

It was her, not Garner, who had it, or knew where it was.

"It's mine, after all" he had snarled, "I planned it all, didn't I?"

Later when he had calmed down and was reporting the incident to Major Havering, Garner reckoned that Rollison was probably on his way to find Freda, if she had survived somewhere.

Little did he know that his arch enemy was to bide his time outside, in the immediate locality, awaiting the Sergeant's next move, and to follow him.

Time would tell.

Chapter 29

A sudden meeting was called by all of the administration at the complex a few days later.

The Major was ordered to report to the meeting where important news was divulged to both him and the senior military leaders by Professor Murdoch and the senior member of the governmental administration, Mrs. Penelope Harris.

The Professor had made a major breakthrough in his search for a vaccine.

Based entirely on the papers and the sample that Garner had acquired from Squires Manor, the Professor was eager to report that just one final and quite small element of the so important formula was still to be tested, but the essential ingredient was not available to him.

He, and his superior, had already passed on the findings to the Americans, Canadians, and European contacts who were excitedly beginning to trial the complete vaccine.

Preliminary reports suggested that the new vaccine could be entirely successful.

But now, to cater for the needs of the UK, the Professor needed to get his hands on the missing ingredient.

'nesta0/27.qig' a rare solution that was believed to be available in a refrigeration unit in the London Hospital vaults.

The solution was to be generally referred to as 'Esther'.

It then fell upon the Major to organise a party to go to London and return with 'Esther'.

Major Havering hurried from the meeting and he called Garner and his NCO, Corporal Les Mason, into his office where they had a three hour long meeting together with the Professor, planning the essentials for the proposed 'errand', as the Major referred to it.

They were to go by helicopter, flown by one of their own pilots.

So after leaving the meeting Garner and a few chosen men drew stores, weapons and ammunition from the stores and loaded all on board the helicopter.

Professor Murdoch and Lizzie loaded a box containing the secret vaccine that he was to supplement with 'Esther' as soon as he obtained it.

They were due to leave as soon as possible, probably late that afternoon.

Garner still sported two black eyes and he had a hard strapping plastered across his face, holding his nose in place.

Lizzie did not look much better with her black eye and split lip.

Corporal Mason and six other ranks, Garner's selected few, and the army pilot, were all well-armed, and all carried the new powerful stun gun.

Liam Murdoch, Lizzie, and Sammy came too.

It was to be the task of the Professor, assisted by Lizzie, to find 'Esther', identify it thoroughly, before using it to complete the finished version of the vaccine, to be known as 'Saviour'.

They were to use the London Hospital's laboratory, and then transport it back to the Dorset complex, after finding that it had 'matured' as expected.

There would be two flasks.

One would contain the new vaccine, 'Saviour'.

And the other would contain a good supply of 'Esther'.

Against military policy Sammy was quietly included for two reasons.

Major Havering had reluctantly agreed with Garner to allow her to go as, since the upsetting incident in the laboratory the youngster had clung to her father and, more importantly, Sammy was showing worrying signs of 'influenza', or very possibly the onslaught of the deadly virus.

So, in a way, the Major had turned a 'blind eye' to the situation and she assisted aboard the helicopter with Lizzie.

Professor Murdoch had his mind set on the job in hand, meaning to spend as little time as was necessary in the hospital laboratory, formulating and completing 'Saviour', and he strapped himself in, next to Lizzie, his face set in an expression of pure concentration.

Outside of the compound Rollison had been roused from a relaxed sleep whilst hiding in thick shrubbery a few yards from the fence.

The sound of the helicopter's rotors whirling brought him to sudden sharp senses and he crept to the fence and watched as Garner and his party boarded the aircraft.

The helicopter took off and after rising slowly to a hundred feet it turned northwards and flew away.

"Damn . . . damn . . . damn . . . ." Rollison muttered angrily, Garner was going away somewhere.

The bastard was avoiding him.

Damn. Damn. Damn.

Just then, now that it had gone quiet, Rollison became aware of someone walking close to the fence, inside the compound, and talking animatedly.

He drew back and lay silently under a gorse bush close to the fence.

Major Havering and his aide were casually strolling along inside the fence, engrossed in deep conversation.

Rollison had very keen hearing and he heard the Major going over the main points of Garner's mission.

And he heard enough to know where the helicopter was heading for.

With the usual evil grin on his face, now filthy after the time spent out in the open, he crept away to where he had hidden the motorbike and, after quietly rolling the bike away to a asphalted lane, he started it up and then roared away, speeding madly in the direction of London.

It was early evening when the helicopter landed on the heli-pad, high on the hospital roof.

Garner led his men across the roof to the entry on the top floor of the building, and the Professor, Lizzie and Sammy were escorted in behind them by the armed helicopter pilot.

It appeared that the building was empty and they were not confronted by anyone by the time that they found the hospital research laboratory on the third floor.

Lizzie and the Professor, with Sammy in tow, searched for 'Esther' first, in the small adjoining storeroom, but were not surprised when they were unsuccessful.

So, leaving Corporal Mason, two soldiers and the army pilot, to stay with Lizzie and Sammy, Garner went with Professor Murdoch and the remaining four soldiers down to the basement area where they found the sealed storeroom that housed the vaults.

The sound of the approaching helicopter had made a group of marauding "Crazies" aware that 'fresh meat' was now somewhere in or near the hospital, and a mob of twenty-eight filthy ragged zombie-like creatures entered the building through the main doors and began to howl as they surged from floor to floor, looking for their prey.

One of Garner's men heard the insane cries of the mob as some of them began to near the head of the stairs leading to the basement area, and he alerted them to the danger.

At that precise moment the Professor, who had just managed to gain entry into an inner sealed unit, something like a huge walk-in safe, and temperature controlled by an independent cooling unit that was still functioning, powered by huge powerful batteries and discovered the vital 'Esther'.

Garner suggested to the Professor that he store the drug in the special flask and that they "Get back upstairs with the others, bloody quick!"

The Professor quickly secured 'Esther' in the flask and then he and the team of armed men began to retrace her steps, knowing full well that they were bound to meet the "Crazies" on the way.

Reaching the top of the first flight of stairs they saw a group of about sixteen ragged men and women approaching.

The group also saw them and they momentarily paused in their race forward.

Then with terrifying screams they started to rush at Garner's small group.

Garner and his men, with the Professor hunched behind them, knelt and aimed the stun weapons at the rushing group and on Garner's order they pulled the triggers.

There was no loud noise from the weapons, simply a soft buzzing sound.

A narrow red laser beam emitted from the muzzle of each gun guiding the user to each target, mainly the head, and instantly all sixteen "Crazies" lay totally unconscious on the floor of the corridor.

"Right. Come on . . . ." Garner ordered, " . . . . let's get back to the others . . . quickly!"

Meanwhile the huge bulky frame of Corporal Mason was filling the doorway of the third floor laboratory entrance, and was about to use his stun-weapon at a second group of "Crazies" coming headlong towards, screaming insanely.

"Shit!" the Corporal exclaimed as the weapon failed to function and before he could react they were upon him.

Fortunately, none of the attackers were armed in anyway, but nevertheless the ferocity of their attack on the big Corporal was fierce.

But 'Big Les', as his comrades affectionately called him, was man enough to deal with them and although he was scratched and torn at he fought them two by two, practically slaying a few by the power of his blows to their heads, he had kept them out.

Then Garner and his group arrived to relieve him, coming up behind the survivors of the Corporals resistance and disposing them with shots fired from their automatic weapons.

Mason was like Garner. He had suffered from the virus in the early days and had survived with immunity to it.

So any contact, including scratches from the sick "Crazies", did not affect him.

Quickly Garner and two other soldiers used their automatic weapons to wipe out the remaining few who had just reached the top of the stairs behind them, leaving it deathly quiet.

Garner then helped to drag the bodies away into a side ward and out of sight.

Lizzie was left to tend to Corporal Mason's wounds and the Professor swiftly used the facilities of the laboratory to prepare the final process of the all important vaccine.

This was completed within the hour but then the Professor informed Garner that an incubation period of six to eight hours must pass before the vaccine could be moved.

Garner posted guards on the essential entry points to the hospital, and he secured those areas that he could not spare men for, by force locking all of the doors and windows.

The Dorset base was contacted by radio and told of the current situation.

They all then relaxed and rested until the vaccine was ready to trial, and to take back to the base.

It was just after midnight that the lanky form of Private Hennessy, who was guarding the stairway up from the basement, heard sounds from below and he whispered his fears by short wave communications to Garner.

"Sarge. I think there's something going on downstairs".

"Like what?"

"I think there's someone moving around down there".

"Do you have any idea how many?"

"No, but they're not trying to be quiet about it. They're quite noisy, Sarge".

"Right. Keep in touch and let me know as soon as they start coming on up" Garner told Hennessy, "Then start shooting. Make a lot of noise and come back up here".

"OK, Sarge". And Hennessy switched off.

The Private was an experienced soldier with many years of service, and he now listened intently for signs of the noise makers getting nearer.

Suddenly, and before he could report back to Garner, a door close by and leading from another corridor burst open and Hennessy was engulfed by a group of seven ragged "Crazies" who quickly overcame him and began to violently tear him to pieces.

The last thing that Private Hennessy was aware of was the inhuman stink of his attackers and the rich coppery odour of his own blood as it spurted copiously from his torn arteries.

The group spent a while ripping at the corpse and feasting on the fresh flesh, studying each other with insane glances as they chewed the tough meat and drank the fruity blood.

Upstairs Garner was becoming worried, as at least fifteen minutes had elapsed since Hennessy had contacted him.

The crazed interlopers now began to claw and fight over the dead soldiers weaponry.

One of them picked up the stun-gun and accidentally pressed the trigger.

Private Hennessy had managed to release the trigger mechanism, preparing to fire the weapon when he was overwhelmed, so now the gun buzzed quietly as it fired.

One of the crazed members was standing in the line of fire and fell silently to the floor.

The leader of this group froze, as did the rest, then realising the power of the weapon he took it, wrestling it from the holder then testing it on him, laughing gleefully as he enjoyed the power that he now held in his hand.

Looking slyly from one to another the leader motioned the weapon threateningly at each one and they, in turn, cringed away from it.

Then the zombie-like leader turned and he signalled for the four remaining "Crazies" to follow him, putting a finger knowingly to his scabbed and split lips, signify that they should be quite.

Garner had been sitting on the laboratory floor, just inside the entrance, trying to contact Private Hennessy on the inter-comms.

He had spoken with the other guards and all appeared OK.

"C'mon, Hennessy, man. Where are you?"

His well-trained senses were sharp and he became tense and he watched carefully along the corridor approach that led to his position.

There was no lighting and only the moonlight flooding through the windows gave any illumination at all.

Strange shadows were cast and Garner squinted through his night lens to look for unusual signs of movement.

Then, just appearing over the top step of the stairway he spotted a definite movement.

Garner gave a low soft whistle to warn the others in the laboratory and he moved low, on his stomach, alongside the partition wall beside the doorway.

The remainder of his party still with him in the laboratory hid quietly behind one of the test benches, out of sight of anyone coming through the doorway.

Garner waited until the creeping group had collected silently some way along the corridor and were gradually nearing the door to the laboratory, and he held his breath and took stock of the ragged individuals.

He was a little confused at first as he could clearly see through the lens that the person leading them at the front was holding one of the new stun-guns.

He suddenly realised now why Hennessy had not been returning his calls, and he aimed at the man's head with his own stun weapon and fired.

The man fell to the floor, the gun clattering loudly on the hard surface.

Ape-like gibbering screams now emitted from the remaining "Crazies" and they hesitated before starting to charge the Sergeant.

Garner aimed and pulled the trigger again, but the weapon needed charging now since it had been used quite a bit earlier, and it buzzed feebly and nothing showed from the muzzle.

Then the crazed four were on him and he managed to draw his SAS knife from it's sheath on his belt and he quickly stabbed two of the stinking, drooling "Crazies" before going under the weight of the last two.

One of them, his clothing still soaking from Hennessy's blood, pressed himself down hard over Garner's head as the other one, a small woman with tremendous strength, tried to wrestle the knife from his hand.

Garner could not see at all and he could barely breathe.

It felt as if his recently broken nose was being moved, very painfully, around his face.

The bloody clothing stifled his breath and pressed hard in between his lips.

He gagged as he tasted thick blood . . . Hennessy's blood, and he began to lose consciousness.

Then they were off of him and he dragged himself up to sit against the wall, gasping for breath and vomiting.

The last two assailants were out cold on the floor and a soldier was dragging them out into the corridor.

Luckily one of his men who had remained with the girls and Professor Murdoch had come to his rescue.

After thanking the soldier Garner ordered him to contact all of the others on their inter-comms. And check if they were OK.

It appeared that only Private Hennessy had perished and all of the others were keeping their posts and had reported everything was quiet and peaceful in their areas.

Garner and a few of the others cleansed themselves thoroughly using disinfectant materials found in the laboratory store.

And Garner spent time gargling and spitting out water in an attempt to rid his mouth of Hennessy's blood and the stench of the "Crazies".

Lizzie tenderly re-sited his loose nose and strapped it firmly with tape that spread across his face.

The remainder of the night passed quietly and in the morning they prepared to leave, waiting the final few hours before the vaccine could be moved.

They were just about to leave, everything packed safely, when there was a huge crashing noise and clamour from the ground floor and the building was suddenly flooded with over forty "Crazies", screaming and baying for flesh and blood.

"Here we go again" Corporal Mason murmured.

Chapter 30

The big Corporal was in the lead as the party evacuated the laboratory area and ascended up to the roof where they intended to fly away as quickly as possible from the madness that hurried through the building, dashing into every room, ward, and every level, searching for their prey.

It was fortunate that poor Sammy could not hear the terrifying screams and the bloodcurdling yells of the "Crazies", for she had worsened overnight and was now in the initial stages of a fever.

Garner felt sick at the thought of his 'little girl' infected with the fatal virus and he had a quiet word with the Professor as the hurried up to the roof, with him and a soldier practically carrying the youngster who appeared totally 'out of it'.

The Professor knew that Sammy was quite likely going down with the virus and he marvelled how she had avoided it so far.

He also knew that if she was not inoculated with the new vaccine soon it could be too late.

They had almost reached the final short stairway to the roof exit when Corporal Mason shouted a warning and they as a group were forced to take cover in an upper control room.

There was a commotion above them and some sort of fight, mirroring what was going on several floors below them as well.

They listened as a multiple of shots were fired and hideous screams rang out before a deathly silence reigned throughout the building.

"OK, you can come out now, if you please. And drop your weapons. Do as you are told and you will not be harmed" a commanding voice, that of a woman, reached them in their area of safety.

"Who are you?" Garner shouted.

"I am Colonel Martha Evans, and I control this region. Do as you are told, please. We will talk later" came the assertive reply.

Suspicious, but sensing that the owner of the voice was of a 'normal' type, Garner commanded his men to leave all of their weapons in the room and follow him up the stairs to the roof where the woman's voice had come from.

Garner had ideas that this 'Colonel' Evans was the leader of a local militia group.

Professor Murdoch, his bag containing the vital vaccine and liquids still across his shoulders, then Lizzie now helping a soldier to assist Sammy along, followed Garner and his men up to the roof where a frightening sight met their eyes.

Inert bodies lay all over the roof area and here and there well-armed personnel stood watching as their leader, a tall powerful looking woman with an authoritative air about her stood with feet apart and hands on her wide hips.

She had what Garner might call a 'Butch' face that exuded a bullishness.

Glaring at Garner's people as they came up from the room below she waited until they had formed a neat group and had assembled before her.

The sight of the helicopter riddled with gunfire and smoking ominously made the Sergeant briefly feel an inner anger which he quickly extinguished sensing a kind of strange caution of this giant of a woman who stood over them.

The helicopter pilot, standing next to Garner emitted a "F***ing hell" when he saw the damage to his aircraft, and Garner nudged him into silence.

Martha Evans was about forty years of age, six feet plus and clearly powerfully built, and with an air of military experience about her.

She looked them over, taking her time to study everyone in turn, but ignoring Lizzie and Sammy who now hung limply in the arms of two soldiers.

She then turned to the helicopter.

"I hope that you did not intend to leave on that today?" she said, then turning to face them again, she demanded, "Who is your leader?"

Garner steeped forward and he automatically saluted her.

"I am, Ma'm. Sergeant Ronald Garner, on an errand for the Provisional Government, Ma'm" he said politely.

"Well, Sergeant. Come with me. The rest of you, except that studious type and the females, help my people to drop these 'things' . . . .", and she said this with deep disgust as she motioned her head in the direction of the bodies, "Drop them over the edge . . . ."

As he followed her, and two of her men who appeared to be her aides, back into the building, Garner saw the bodies being lifted and swung out over the edge of the roof where they were released to fall to the ground far below, even though a few were not quite dead.

In the control room where they had sheltered just minutes ago, Martha Evans sat behind the controllers big desk with one of her aides beside her, and the other standing to Garner's left and just behind him.

Now the Sergeant could smell the strong odour of the woman's unwashed body, although the man close to him definitely was wearing some expensive after-shave.

"Right, now, Sergeant" she began, leaning on her folded arms and staring belligerently at him, "I rule this area with a rod of iron. Take no prisoners. So anything that goes on around here I know about".

She was obviously obsessed with her own assumed power.

Power-mad, Garner was thinking, but not caused by any virus.

"What is this errand you spoke of?" she enquired.

And before he could answer she leant back, closing her eyes and offering up her reason for 'taking charge'.

"I was in the army. Yes, I enjoyed twelve active years. Reached the heady rank of Sergeant, like yourself" she told him, "They chucked me out . . . . ten years ago . . . on some trumped up charge. You know how it is sometimes. Quite unfair. Quite unfair" she repeated.

She then seemed to wake from her ramblings, "Anyway, I have organised this group of men, and a few women, into a strong and able unit. Well drilled and very able and willing to kill those sick animals roaming around out there".

"I believe that I can handle most situations in my region" she added.

"Your region, Ma'm?" Garner asked her politely.

"Yes, Sergeant. My region." She answered then looked around at the aide standing near her, "We reckon we control an area of ten miles around here"

The aide answered obediently, "Yes, Colonel. We have full control for many miles" he said.

Full control? Garner was thinking.

Why, they had not shown any control of the scores of "Crazies" that had managed to roam the area and attack within the hospital last night, and this morning.

As she spoke he could see a shining glint of mania in her black eyes.

Then, repeating her earlier question, "What manner of an errand were you on, Sergeant? And who is this Provisional Government you speak of?" and she said this with scorn in her voice.

Garner explained first the complex in Dorset, and then the authority there, describing the levels of seniority, military ranks and government ministerial levels that had survived and were communicating with other nations.

Colonel Evans scoffed, she then ordered Garner to continue.

He told her of the vital need for the vaccine and that their visit to the hospital was simply to procure an ingredient necessary to complete a vaccine which was considered a possible solution to the killer virus.

To this Martha Evans had listened intently, an obvious mass of thoughts racing through her mind.

"And do you have it?" she asked.

Garner decided to play safe. "No, not quite, Ma'm" he replied, and thinking quickly he said, "We need to get to another hospital first" he lied.

Martha looked at him, her eyes squinting as if she was considering his honesty.

"What other hospital?" she asked.

Thinking quickly again Garner named a major hospital local to where his home had been.

"Queen Mary's, Sidcup, Ma'm" he said, still standing stiffly at attention and directing his eyes straight at her.

"Why would they keep such a drug there?" Martha was quick to ask.

"I believe it was transferred there together with other major elements and chemicals as a safe store when things began to "blow up" in London". Garner offered, hoping that she would now believe him.

She studied his face with her squinting pig-like eyes and then she suddenly accepted his explanation as the truth.

She pushed back the chair she was sitting in and stood up, leaning on her curled fingers pressed down on the desk top.

"Well you had better get on with it, Sergeant" she stated, her voice taking on a commanding tone.

Garner saluted, "Yes, Ma'm" he said.

"I think that maybe you should take a few of my people with you to give you extra firepower". She added, causing him to hesitate.

She had run her eyes over the weapons, stacked in a corner by Garner's group earlier.

Martha Evans signalled to the aide standing near Garner.

"Bring me one of those weird looking things" she said and she pointed at the new stun guns.

The aide took one to her.

She handled it with curiosity on her face.

"What is this? Tell me about this?" she said, looking up at Garner.

Garner stepped up to the desk and described the function of the newly designed weapon and that it was being tested in the field.

He emphasised that it was early days and that it required constant recharging and so far he had found it unreliable.

"If I help you, can you get your superiors to supply me with a stock of these?" Martha asked him, still studying the weapon in her hands.

"I can try . . . ." Garner offered.

Corporal Mason was called into the control room together with the soldier carrying the long distance communications pack.

Martha nodded to Garner and he contacted the Dorset base.

Major Havering was called to take the call and after Garner had explained the reason for this call he handed the handset to Martha Evans.

Some discussion followed and she was diplomatically informed that although she held no recognised rank she would be issued with a supply of the stun-guns and the relevant associated equipment needed to support them.

These would be convoyed to her the next day, and Major Havering kept her 'sweet' by praising her for her courage and the work she was doing in her area, and that he would consider that his superiors might accept her rank.

This seemed to please her, although at first she had grudgingly agreed, but then the Majors flattery had altered her demeanour.

So finally Garner and his party were allowed to prepare to leave, watched closely by one of the female Colonel's aides.

Garner had quietly taken Professor Murdoch aside and had managed to warn him of his 'white lie' regarding the vaccine that they had already, and he hinted that they might 'lose' their escort if possible once they had reached the Queen Mary Hospital in Sidcup.

Colonel Evans stood with her well-armed group and she saluted Garner as he led his party early that afternoon, accompanied by six of her followers, four men and two women.

She had found them two vehicles to use, one of them previously used as a delivery van for a well-known DIY store, and the other was an ambulance.

It took over four hours to get to North Kent as many of the London streets were damaged or strewn with a mass of vehicles left by their owners as they panicked, and then had attempted to flee the London area.

Also they managed to avoid clashing with any of the many groups of "Crazies" as the afternoon wore on, for the weather had become oppressively hot and the poor demented creatures had sought cool places to rest.

Shadowing the two vehicles, and staying well out of sight, Rollison followed them although he was now somewhat quite tired after yesterday's race to the London Hospital, and the subsequent waiting in the shadows, witnessing the mob madness and then the bodies falling from the roof of the hospital, before Garner and his team emerged to begin their journey.

He had witnessed the big woman who appeared to be in authority and had saluted as Garner's convoy moved off.

He had no idea of what was going on but he meant to keep Garner in his sights.

So it was early evening when at last the two vehicles arrived at the main entrance of the Queen Mary Hospital, in Sidcup.

As usual the whole area appeared totally deserted with no sign of any corpses anywhere.

Martha Evan's mixed crew had grown tired and lazy as the journey had progressed and it became very easy for Corporal Mason and two of Garner's men to disarm them.

The six were herded into an empty reception room and locked in with a guard outside the door.

Garner radioed base to tell them of his position and the action that he had taken with the motley crew from Martha Evans militia, and he was told to sit tight for the night and then make his way together with his party back to base.

He was also instructed to offer Martha Evans people the chance to join a 'real' professional outfit before he left.

Garner did this, going directly to the room where the six were imprisoned and he invited them to serve with him for the Provisional Government.

He left them to consider the offer and was called back after they had a brief meeting, all of them deciding to join with Garner.

Garner took them to a canteen area where they were given food and supplied with weapon each. They all appeared very pleased at this new future offered them.

Sammy had become worse during the journey from London and the Professor made her comfortable in a small one-bed ward on the ground floor.

He took Garner aside and warned him of the seriousness of Sammy's health.

Seeing tears in Garner's eyes the Professor suggested that there could be a real chance for her if he was allowed to administer the newly formed vaccine to her.

It was a chance.

The new vaccine had not been proven in any way yet, although it was considered by the Professor and his peers that it was expected to be the real solution to the virus.

"It may be her only chance, Ron" Liam Murdoch said in a friendly tone.

The two men had grown close, respect and friendship now being the order of the day.

Worried sick, Garner battled with himself to agree, finally getting the Professor's promise that he would do all possible tests first.

Blood tests were taken from the youngster and very soon the Professor confirmed that Sammy was in the initial stage of the infection.

Once more the two men discussed the situation.

"I cannot promise one hundred per cent that the vaccine will prevent the virus from making Samantha worse, but I do have some confidence in it, and as I said before, Ron, it may be her only chance" the Professor emphasised again.

Garner shook his head. "Go ahead, Doc". He said, and the Professor left to go directly to Sammy and inject her with the initial dose of the untried vaccine.

Garner stayed, sitting beside his daughter as she lay in a deep feverish slumber.

He held her damp hand and gently wiped her damp forehead with a cool cloth that Lizzie had wet under a cold tap.

Finally she appeared to become calmer and slept deeply.

Garner left Lizzie to watch over his daughter and walked the ground floor area, checking on his men, at their posts, before he sat with the Professor and Corporal Mason, discussing plans for the following day.

The three men talked for almost an hour and it was dark outside.

Garner left the two men resting and he walked back to the small ward to check on Sammy.

He knew that something was wrong as he neared the room and he started to run along the dark corridor.

The door was closed, just as he had left it earlier, but upon entry he saw that the bed was empty and the window was open wide.

And worse still . . . . Sammy and Lizzie were gone!

Chapter 31

It had been just minutes before, when the window to the small ward silently opened.

A cool draft filtered across the room and Lizzie, who was sitting beside the bed where the youngster was quietly sleeping, heard the soft sounds and she felt the air movement.

A sudden fearful chill swept the nape of her neck.

She slowly turned her head towards the window, not really knowing what to expect.

Rollison put his index finger to his lips commanding Lizzie's silence, and he swept the room with a hand-gun.

Satisfied that the girls were alone he spoke in soft deep tones.

"Get her up . . . c'mon . . . now . . . over here. You're both coming with me".

And he motioned her towards the window.

Petrified with utter fear of this man Lizzie stammered, "She's very ill".

"I don't give a shit. Get the brat up . . . . NOW!" Rollison rasped, his voice just enough to menace the nurse.

Rollison had a dark mad stare in his eyes, and his snarling teeth appeared animal-like.

Lizzie, shaking with fear, urged Sammy from her slumber and into a slowly waking state.

The nurse helped the girl to move out of the bed and onto her bare feet.

Unsteadily Sammy leant hard into Lizzie as she was guided over to the window where Rollison cruelly hooked an arm around the youngster and dragged her roughly through the window.

Sammy was hauled up onto Rollison's wide shoulders and her night dress caught on a window stop and a piece was ripped off.

He waved the gun in Lizzie's face, "C'mon, bitch . . . get out here . . . now. Or this little cow gets it".

Lizzie climbed awkwardly out of the window, her legs showing bare up to her thighs.

Rollison grinned, and he licked his lips. "Oh, yeah . . . ." He whispered huskily.

It was a very humid night and the strong fragrance of nearby shrubs filled their lungs.

Lizzie was shoved violently as Rollison guided her away from the building.

He was hurrying her towards the perimeter of the hospital where a road lay.

Sammy, still quite affected by the injection that had been administered earlier, was somewhat unaware of their plight and she moaned softly as she lay across Rollison's shoulders.

Then they were suddenly at the roadside and the dark shape of a stationery van stood near.

Rollison opened the sliding door at the side of the vehicle and he slung the limp form of the youngster roughly into the back, motioning with the gun for Lizzie to follow.

As Lizzie climbed up into the van she felt his hand slide up her leg before pushing her by her buttocks so that she fell across Sammy who lay weeping quietly on the floor.

He then slid the door closed and Lizzie heard the sound of a latch or lock clicking shut.

By now Garner had climbed out of the window, his heart racing for fear of the unknown danger that he imagined the girls could be in.

He had seen the torn piece of night dress and he feared for their safety.

Garner stood, straining to hear any sounds that might lead him to them.

There.

He thought that he heard the sound of tyres on a gritty surface.

Racing through the shrubbery he headed for the sound realising that it was becoming fainter.

He had briefly considered returning for assistance but was too concerned for Sammy and Lizzie and he raced onwards suddenly coming out of the greenery and skidding to a stop on a dark road.

There was a full moon with scudding clouds drifting across the night sky and, in the bright moonlight Garner saw, rolling on a downward slope, the dark shape of a van that was now some hundred yards or more distant.

Suddenly the vehicle's engine was started and it sped quickly away, down the empty dual carriageway that led towards the M20 motorway.

There was nothing that Garner could do as he saw the van, with no lights on, disappearing in the distance.

His heart in his mouth he raced back, hell for leather, to the hospital.

One of his men stood alert as he saw Garner rushing towards him.

"Quick. Get Mason and a few men. Grab a vehicle and follow me" he shouted the order to the man.

He jumped into the Ambulance that they had used to get to the hospital, started it up and roared out of the hospital grounds.

Driving out he took the slip road that led on to the A20 driving in the direction that the dark van had taken.

As he drove, his training crept into his tortured mind and he forced himself to think rationally.

He had not turned on the ambulance's lights for fear of his quarry knowing of his pursuit, and he decided to continue to drive unlit.

Garner knew that when the soldier reported his instructions to Corporal Mason they would follow and probably be well lit up, but they would be quite some distance behind and he hoped that he would be closer to his quarry by then.

All that he could surmise was that the girls had been taken for a reason.

Thinking, he found that it made sense that his old foe, Rollison, was involved, and was probably using the girls as bait to get him to divulge where the sought after 'treasure' was.

But how had Rollison got here?

How had he known?

How did he travel?

It seemed quite unbelievable.

It was insane that the man still lusted for their ill-gotten gains in this dark period of the world's history, and when many other riches were for the taking, just like Samuel Rogers had been doing when he was apprehended.

But Rollison had always been a strange one who, once fixed on an intention would follow it through no matter who got hurt on the way.

Garner peered ahead.

Yes, there it was.

The van.

Still haring southwards.

Then suddenly it veered to the left and shot up the side road that led to the intersection with the M25 Motorway, the London Orbital Motorway.

Following, Garner found that they were now heading for the Dartford crossing and he knew then that if the van turned off onto the London bound A2 then it would certainly be Rollison, and he would undoubtedly be heading for Garner's old home in Sidcup.

Some miles behind, Corporal Mason led all of the personnel from the hospital, including their new recruits, in the remaining vehicle and soon after the darkened van, and then the Sergeant, had left the A20, he and the others hurtled past, continuing South Eastwards towards the M20, and the Kent coast.

With no method of communication between the small group of soldiers and Garner they were to discover much later of their wild goose chase, and they were to stop to consider all alternatives.

Meanwhile Garner pursued the van as it veered left just as he had suspected, and he followed at a reasonable distance as they raced towards London, and the sleepy suburb of Sidcup.

Chapter 32

By now Garner was beginning to feel the effects of the very little sleep that he had managed to get during the recent forty-eight hours.

He steered automatically, concentrating hard to keep the target vehicle within his sight.

His eyes smarted and prickled with tiredness, and he shook his head a number of times in an attempt to keep himself from closing his eyes and giving in to exhaustion.

But each time he shook his head it felt as if his broken nose was floating, and it hurt like hell.

As if to goad and to tempt him, the van in front now had its lights on and the sudden bright glimmer of the rear lights shook Garner from his enveloping stupor.

He eased back and he concentrated on staying at a distance meant to puzzle his prey, but he knew deep inside that, if it was Rollison, and he felt sure that it was and then it was he who was the one being led and duped into whatever his old adversary had planned for him and the girls.

At last, just as he had expected he found himself about to drive down the road where he had once lived.

Where he, Sammy and Lizzie, had spent those earlier days after his freedom from prison and before their recent adventures had begun.

He slowed to a halt and parked around the corner, and watched as the van drew up outside his house.

He saw the dark figure, tall and wielding a weapon, motion the two girls from the back of the van.

Garner's heart leapt as he saw Lizzie holding up the frail figure of his daughter as Rollison ushered them up to the house.

Tears were in his eyes as he watched them go into the house and, after a fleeting look around outside, Rollison closed the door.

Pondering his next move, and watching as the trio disappeared into the house, Garner was suddenly shaken from his stupor by the sound of gunshots and screams of pain and terror that came from inside the house.

Panicking and flushed with a terrible fear and horror that Sammy, and Lizzie, had been hurt, or even worse killed, Garner grabbed his Uzi machine gun from the front seat and slammed out of his vehicle, running without any real concern for his own safety towards the darkened house.

He was now running on adrenalin for his mind and body was close to exhaustion, but he forced himself to move automatically in his attempt to get to the two people who meant everything to him.

Running into the hallway he was met by the sight of two bodies spread across the floor of the lounge, blood streaming freshly from the terrible gunshot wounds that had cut them down and running in rivulets into the carpet.

Choking with the pain of sudden grief he bent to check each one only to find that both were "Crazies", and both were young females, their awful smelling bodies now twitching in the dying throes of death.

Then.

"In here, old chap. Do come in" The sardonic tones of Rollison's voice reached him from a dark corner of the lounge.

Garner stepped into the dark room, his eyes searching for his enemy.

He made out the dark shadowy figure in the corner and he began to raise his weapon to shoot.

"I wouldn't do that, old bean" he heard Rollison from a distance as his exhausted brain caused him to ease on the trigger.

"I have your treasured daughter and bit of skirt here, and I will shoot them. You know I will". Rollison threatened.

Brokenly Garner lowered his weapon and he stood head bowed waiting for the next command.

"Drop that silly Uzi, old chap, and come towards me. Slowly now"

Garner did as Rollison instructed, his tired mind struggling to stay alert, searching for some way out of this mess, and of saving the girls from any danger or injury that this madman threatened.

"That's it . . . good . . . good . . . come on in. That's a good chap." Rollison goaded him, "See. It's easy when you do as you're told".

Garner staggered a little.

He was able to see Sammy being held protectively by Lizzie as they crouched in the bay window area.

"You OK?" he managed to croak, his question directed to them.

Lizzie nodded but Sammy remained in a comatose state in the nurse's embrace.

"What have you done to her, you evil bastard?" Garner stepped towards the dark figure in the corner.

Rollison chuckled.

"Hey. Steady on. Don't forget who's holding all the cards now".

Then "Get down. On your knees. NOW!? Rollison suddenly became violently threatening.

Garner dropped to his knees.

Rollison stepped out of the shadows and stood before Garner.

He pressed the muzzle of his rifle to Garner's forehead.

"Now, old bean. At last. Tell me where our beautiful prize is. Come on. Tell me".

Garner turned his haggard features up to his adversary.

"I don't know" he rasped, sweat dripping from his brow and tears now running from his eyes. "I really don't know".

Rollison looked down at him in disbelief and he forced Garner's head back as he exerted pressure with the rifle.

"Don't lie to me!" he screamed with an insane rage, "I know you had it. You were the last one to handle it. You took it home, didn't you!"

Garner's head dropped in surrender, "Yes. I took it home. But it had gone . . . disappeared . . . before I was picked up by the police . . . ."

"Liar!" Rollison screamed, and turning the rifle quickly he slammed the stock into the side of Garner's head.

The Sergeant fell sideways to the floor. Out cold.

Lizzie, crouching beside Sammy by the bay window, started to move forward towards Garner.

"Stay!" Rollison growled at her, "Leave him".

He strode over to the window and Lizzie drew Sammy away from him as he pulled the curtains to one side and checked the immediate surroundings.

Nothing.

No one there.

No more "Crazies" anyway.

Rollison turned once again to his captives.

Lizzie trembled in fear as she recognised the evil look of lust in his snake-like eyes.

With his familiar cold sneering smile, his big toothy grin on his face, he approached her.

"Right" he began, "What shall we do while we wait for old sleepy head to wake up?"

Lowering the rifle, Rollison stepped closer to the nurse.

Lizzie shrank back, trying to mould herself deeper into the dark corner of the bay.

She whimpered with fear as she realised that there was nowhere to go.

She was trapped.

Helpless.

He bent over her and grabbed her by the upper arm.

"C'mere, you sexy bitch" he chuckled evilly.

He began to pull her to her feet.

He stopped, and looked around the room.

There had been a sound.

Of what?

Where?

Shoving Lizzie back down beside the youngster he turned swiftly and moved over to the partly open front door.

Rollison stood beside the opening and he peered around the edge of the door into the dimness outside.

Dawn was now beginning to spread it's faded light across the sky and the street was starting to become more discernible.

A rustling noise came again.

From within the house.

Rollison turned quickly and he heard the sounds coming from behind the cupboard door that led to the area under the stairs.

Then, just as he began to move towards the cupboard the door flew open and a most terrible looking spectre burst from within, emitting the most horrifying screech he had ever heard.

Rollison started to raise his weapon but the figure, clad entirely in filthy and stained black robes and hood, lashed out with something that he had not seen and his rifle was knocked from his hands.

The figure paused before him and it raised its head.

The dawn light lit up the skeletal features, a face of pure evil, with green/yellow pus oozing from many sores.

The eyes were deep set and surrounded by very dark circles, but the eyes themselves gleamed brightly with a terrible madness.

Chapter 33

Corporal Mason and the others were moving back towards London, along the M20.

He had realised that Garner and his quarry must have left the motorway earlier.

The vehicle stopped on the hard shoulder and Corporal Mason and the Professor discussed their options.

Both were wondering if Rollison could be involved, knowing that there was always that threat to Garner and Sammy.

But also wondering how the man could have known their whereabouts.

"What if you speak to Major Havering?" the Professor suggested.

Mason considered the idea.

"Well I reckon that they've turned eastwards. Sergeant Garner once lived somewhere in that direction and if it was that maniac Rollison he was chasing then they would be aiming for his home, or maybe somewhere nearby".

He fingered his chin thoughtfully.

"The Sergeant did mention once that Rollison was obsessed with obtaining something he thought he still had . . . ."

"Would the Major know of Sergeant Garner's old home address?" asked the Professor.

"Probably. He's got records. I'll try him", and Mason instructed their radio operator to contact base.

Maybe. Just maybe, that was the way to go.

He hoped so.

Back at the house the spectre had stopped screeching and it stood swaying from side to side, wailing softly as its bright insane eyes rested on the still form of young Sammy.

Then the inhuman wailing was interrupted as young Sammy started to moan.

Rollison, his own eyes protruding in fear, stopped backing away from the awful figure before him.

He had seen it before.

It was the mad Nun that he had seen during his time trailing Garner through the Southern counties.

This time he was so close to her . . . the mad Nun!

The strong smell of her body odour and the mix of stale blood and vomit on her robes gave him a sudden feeling of nausea.

The mad woman then raised her head and she snarled as she looked over towards the youngster, and with a speed and agility that belied her, she raised the long blade and another of her guttural shrieks emitted from her throat.

Rollison came out of his rigid stance and he bent quickly to retrieve the rifle, raising it and hitting the Nun across the back with it.

The woman dived uncontrollably, falling unconscious across the still figure of Garner, the Samurai sword that she had taken from the cottage in Lulworth crashing to the floor beside them.

The falling body roused the Sergeant from his coma-like state and he opened his eyes.

God. His head hurt.

It was bloodied where Rollison's rifle butt had split his scalp.

Garner groaned and he retched at the stench of the heavy robes that had fallen across his face.

He shoved at the body, pushing it from him, and he started to sit up.

"So . . . . , the hero is back with us" he heard Rollison say sarcastically.

Garner lay propped up on his elbows with the inert form of the filthy Nun lying beside him.

She appeared to be dead.

Rollison poked her body hard with his rifle, the muzzle pressing into her stomach.

"Mad Cow" he sneered, then as he turned to continue his tortuous interrogation of Garner, a hand grabbed at his ankle and it pulled firmly.

Losing his balance he fell backwards.

Garner had taken the opportunity to unbalance the man and now, having gathered enough strength, he threw himself on Rollison and his hands clutched at the man's throat.

They fought ferociously, crashing across the room, sending furniture and ornaments flying as they used all of their SAS training to gain advantage over each other.

Rollison brought his knee up and rammed it hard into Garner's crotch.

Tears welled again in the Sergeants eyes and he gasped, loosening his grip, and Rollison easily turned them both so that it was he who was now on top.

The two grappled fiercely, and Rollison managed to draw his wicked looking sheath knife from his belt.

Raising it high he targeted Garner's throat.

Garner caught and held the wrist.

Rollison grinned evilly and he used his weight and his strength to slowly direct the point of the knife to the Sergeants neck and upper body.

Somehow, summoning up all of the remaining strength in his tired and strained muscles Garner managed to redirect the knife, but it sliced easily and deep into his left shoulder.

He screamed with pain, his face screwing up in agony, but the sudden pain caused a repeat of his adversary's earlier action, and it was Garner who now brought up a knee to smash it hard into his assailants groin.

Again they rolled and Garner pushed back, getting to his knees with blood flowing from the wound in his shoulder.

Unseen by the two men, totally engrossed in their hatred and the fight, the Nun had regained consciousness and she now stood swaying unsteadily over them, blood trickling from her temple, her samurai sword back in her hands.

Rollison was now on his back, and he had recovered his rifle.

With a snarl of pure hatred on his face he raised the weapon and he aimed it at Garner.

This was the moment when everything seemed to freeze.

The Nun had wailed loudly, a horrible animal-like cry, and Sammy, who was now awake had cried out a strangled, "Mummmmmmyyyy . . . ."

Garner looked up at the Nun who was now staring at Sammy as she held the sword high above her head.

Rollison stared incredulously from Garner to the Nun.

Both men gasped with a sudden realisation.

"Freda?"

The Nun turned her ugly ravaged face and she looked first at Garner.

Her expression of hate softened, then hardened again as she turned her eyes to meet Rollison's look of complete surprise.

He saw at once the hate there and he turned the rifle, aiming it now at the mad woman's chest.

She shrieked a piercing scream and lifted the samurai sword high with both hands.

Rollison fired.

One shot.

The bullet hit the Nun high up in the chest.

She momentarily staggered, and then with an insane grin on her face she once again raised the sword higher above her head.

Rollison fired again.

And once again the shot hit her high in the chest.

She stood rocking on her heels, blood now running from the corner of her gaping mouth.

Then, as her eyes started to glaze over, death beckoning, she used all of her failing strength and will power and she brought the sword down, double handed, driving the point into Rollison's upper stomach, and forcing it fully into him with her falling body.

Garner rolled aside as the Nun fell across Rollison who now choked up blood before relaxing back in the throes of death.

Garner scrambled over to the Nun.

He turned her over, not believing what he was about to discover.

Lizzie was assisting young Sammy who for some reason now started to crawl over to her father and the Nun.

The woman was dying.

She gave them both a tired smile, and she tried to find something within the folds of her robes.

Puzzled, Garner and the girls watched as the Nun drew from her clothing a dirty soft leather pouch.

Garner cried softly, tears again welling in his eyes.

It was the bag containing the ill-gotten gains that Rollison had insanely pursued.

With difficulty the dying woman raised the small pouch, offering it to Garner, but then with her last act she swung her hand around and pushed the pouch into Rollison's gaping bloody mouth.

She then twitched a couple of times, then died, falling limply alongside Rollison who now was gagging and choking blood before he too relaxed and death took him.

Holding each other tightly, on their knees, Garner and Sammy looked at the face of his wife, he mother, who now in death had a softer expression on her face ravaged by the terrible virus.

Lizzie helped them both to their feet and all three embraced, sobbing with relief and shock.

The pain in his head, crotch, and shoulder made Garner feel quite weak but he held the girls tightly.

"Now it's over. I'll never leave you. Both of you. Oh, God, how I love you" he exclaimed with tears running down his battered face.

From outside the house there now came the sounds of a vehicle screeching to a halt, and then the slamming of doors.

Hob-nailed boots clattered up the driveway and into the house.

Corporal Mason, followed by Professor Murdoch, came rushing in.

The rest of the squad, including the new recruits, pushed into the house behind them.

They all stopped dead and they surveyed the scene before them.

The Professor crossed the room to check on Sammy, his very important patient, who seemed to have proven that the new vaccine that he had tried on her had worked perfectly, and she was very much improved despite all that had happened.

Garner stood, assisted by Lizzie who held him tightly.

The big Corporal came over to them and he put a hand on Garner's uninjured shoulder.

"All sorted then, Sarge" he said with a smile.

The End